MY DEAR BOY

MY DEAR BOY

Kim Joonmin

To order additional copies of this book, contact:
Xlibris
1-888-795-4274
www.Xlibris.com
Orders@Xlibris.com
813168

CHAPTER 1

Woken up by the sound of my alarm blaring next to my head, sleepily, I reached out from under the covers and tried to locate the alarm clock. A few thuds and a loud crash later, I finally managed to turn it off. I groaned as I sat up scratching my head and stretching. Smacking my lips together to get rid of my cottonmouth— I reached over to pick up my phone, watch, and a book I'd successfully knocked on the floor in my earlier quest.

Glancing around the small room in a half dazed sleep, I knew it was time to clean my pig sty of a living space. The dishes were stacked a mile high in the kitchen sink, as I hadn't had the energy to clean them. On the small worn out foldable surface I dared to call my dining table, was a half dead plant that I had neglected. A trail of dirty clothes leading from the front door straight to the bed was a reminder of just how exhausting yesterday truly was. The dust in the air shimmered as it floated through the ray of sunlight coming in from the only window, located next to the bed. I yawned widely as I blinked the sleep out of my eyes.

Moving on autopilot, I habitually made the bed— smoothing out every wrinkle, and placing the pillow right in the center. With a still tired smile, I placed Mr. Snuggles— a dark brown teddy bear wearing a light brown sweater— on his pillow throne. Content, I wobbled into the bathroom.

With my hair a mess and my eyes barely open, I turned on the blue bluetooth speaker, hit the 'favorites' playlist, and began getting ready for the day. Shambling like a zombie I slowly brushed my teeth, then took a shower.

Finally fully awake, I dressed in a pair of black slacks, a plain white tee-shirt, and black socks. I slid into the kitchen, dancing to 'Boy' by Anne-Marie as I put two pieces of bread in the toaster, and towel dried my hair. Another alarm started to ring, interrupting the song, letting me know it was time to leave. With a frown, I silenced the noise as the toaster popped up my breakfast. Quickly spreading strawberry jam on the toast, I hurried out the door.

As soon as I walked down the stairs of my apartment complex, I plugged in my headphones. Pulling up the hood of my jacket, I noticed I'd forgotten gloves. I hurriedly checked the time with a sharp inhale, then decidedly shoved my hands into my pockets.

"It should be fine," I thought as I made my way to the main street.

Stepping off the bus, I instantly locked my eyes on the sidewalk to avoid the judgemental stares of everyone around me as I made my way through the main street to the bakery. Noticing a large group of people out of the corner of my eye, I quickly moved aside actively trying to avoid them by moving closer to the incoming traffic; so close the wind from the cars blew off my hood. Even so, I still managed to get bumped by a stranger who suddenly staggered out of the group of people walking down the center of the sidewalk. With his disheveled appearance, you could tell he hadn't slept properly in days. I instinctively reached out and grabbed his arm to stop myself from falling into the street, but as I grabbed him... I saw it.

I saw exactly how he was going to die.

In the same disheveled appearance, he was standing at a crosswalk full of people. As he reached over and repeatedly hit the button to change the light, he seemed to grow more impatient as the cars continued to drive past. Anxiously, he glanced down at his watch, then groaned again and throws his hand down in frustration. He ran his hands through his greasy hair, groaning even louder as his patients appears to finally run out. Taking one more quick glance at his watch, he briefly looked around, and stepped into the onslaught of moving cars. As he scurries into the road, he glanced one way, then the other, somehow missing the small white car that inevitably mows him down. With a gasp, I let him go instantly.

"I'm so sorry!" the man exclaimed distractedly, "I'm in a hurry. Excuse me."

"Be careful crossing the street," I muttered breathlessly as I turned away from him. The man scoffed at me, annoyed as he continued on his way. Aware that he was going to ignore me, I turned back around to follow him, but he was already gone.

My visions do not tell me exactly when a person will die; they simply tell me how. With this thought and a deep breath, I turned back around and started to walk away. Suddenly there was a loud screech, followed by a crash and a woman's blood curdling scream, coming from the corner behind me. I rushed toward the crowd, elbowing my way through the people. I could hear my heartbeat pounding in my ears, followed by my gasps for breath as I finally made it to the curb. I forced myself to look up, and just as I feared— lying in the street behind a small white car with his head cracked wide open— was the man I just bumped into.

"I told you," I whispered as the life left his eyes.

"Do you know him?" came the sound of a voice that snapped me back to reality.

"Ah. . . no. No I don't," I stated, just a little too coldly, as I threw up my hood and carefully pushed my way back through the crowd.

"Wait! Hang on," shouted the voice as he tried to follow me, but the accident had gathered too much attention from onlookers, allowing me to slip away.

My name is Park-Chul Joon, and when I have physical contact with someone— I can see how that person will die

Standing hunched over in a dark corner of an alley next to a trash can, I hurled my guts out— which only added to the pain of my body feeling like it just got run over by a car because not only can I see how a person will die, I also feel it physically and emotionally— as if I am the one who is dying. It's only *slightly* inconvenient. "Tsk. I knew I should have gone back for my gloves," I muttered as I wiped my mouth. With my new headache, I shoved my hands into my pockets, looked down at my feet, and continued walking.

"Guess I'm going to be late to work again," I exasperatedly sighed.

"HEY," shouted my manager Mr. Wei as I walked into the small bakery building from the alley entrance.

"WHERE HAVE YOU BEEN," he continues to shout.

"Aw~aw, why do you always have to shout?" I whined with my hands covering my ears.

"Because you are always late, you stinkin' punk!" he grunts through his teeth, taking a swing at the back of my head.

With just enough time— I ducked his swing and showed my hands, revealing a pair of black cotton gloves.

"Had to get a new pair of gloves," I said with a smile, "forgot mine at home."

Mr. Wei rolled his eyes as we walked down the cramped employee hallway. "You're just lucky you have an amazing talent, or I would have fired your ass a long time ago," Mr. Wei said in his most convincing stern voice.

"Awe come on Mr. Wei, I could never leave— even if you paid me to," I replied sweetly as I snuck around him.

"You know we have extra gloves here, no need to waste your money on buying new ones," He chided shaking his head.

"Aw, but I like adding new gloves to my collection," I chuckled m wriggling my fingers to show off.

"Yeah, yeah" he said, brushing off the excuse, "just get to work, will ya?"

"Of course." I answered with a slight bow, walking through the door into the kitchen.

Mr. Wei just shook his head as the door closed behind me. I sighed a heavy sigh, cutting through the kitchen to get to the employees' locker room.

A ding rang from the front door as it opened, and a tall young man with dark brown hair and large brown eyes walked in. Wearing a pair of pants with giant holes in the knees, a grey shirt that had a large smiley face emoji on it, and a red varsity jacket. In contrast, following him were three men dressed in suits, with pitch black sunglasses and earpieces in their right ears.

The man casually walks around the bakery, admiring all the deserts behind the seemingly endless glass counters that lined all but one wall. In the center of the bakery is a display of all the fresh bread available labeled by the many different types. On the wall that doesn't have a glass case full of deserts has a large window that looks into the kitchen instead. And placed, as if on purpose, right beside the window was the dining area for customers. Mostly filled with young women the customers had a full view of the kitchen but more importantly a full view of the pâtissiers.

Noticing the sudden onslaught of squeals and giggles coming from the gaggle of female customers he looked up from the glass cake cases. Through the window a handsome young man wearing a white chef hat could be seen standing intensely looking at a blank cake not moving a muscle. He had straight short solid black hair with bangs that barely hung over his light baby blue eyes. Dressed in all white his hair looked like a dark starless night and his eyes looked like a bright clear morning sky. Standing arms crossed slowly raising his right hand to his face rubbing his bottom lip ever so slightly with his thumb as he continued to ponder on the design.

Intrigued he stopped and stared as the man's eyes suddenly lit up and he began to decorate the cake. The man began to make flowers of all different colors and sizes effortlessly as if he could complete the task with his eyes closed. Gracefully he added one flower after another as if he didn't even have to think about where the flowers were being placed. With the slightest flick of his wrist he would spin the cake and place another flower ever so gently. Completely entranced from the look of concentration on the young man's face to the effortless piping of the frosting. He couldn't help but stare.

He spins the cake as he takes a step back bringing his hand with the scissors covered in frosting close to his face. Gently he used his thumb to rub his bottom lip while looking at the cake. The tip of the scissors lightly touched his cheek leaving a trace of the butter crème on his pale skin. Putting the scissors down he immediately continues to decorate the cake leaving the butter crème on his cheek. Grabbing a piping bag he begins piping long skinny ropes of buttercream frosting on the sides of the cake with a steady smooth hand that only stops to turn the cake. With a small pair of tweezers he grabs smaller flowers which had been on the counter and began placing them sporadically on the sides. Spinning the cake every so often to find the empty spaces.

Right as the pâtissier was about to finish decorating a happy, innocent and adorable smile appeared across his face as he placed the final flower. The smile instantly faded as the man suddenly looked up from the cake and noticed the crowd of people staring at him. Looking directly into the man's eyes they were prettier than he originally thought. As if completely lost in the light blue color he continued to stare until a bodyguard let out a soft cough. Then as if he was caught red handed doing something wrong he shyly looked away from the window and continued to look at the cakes around the bakery. With a quick glance back towards the window he saw the pâtissier had left and with a disappointed sigh he looked away.

"Ah Chairman Lan you are here!" Mr. Wei said as he walked out of his office.

"Please Chairman Lan was my father, call me Min-jah, no need to be so formal" he said with a gentle smile as he stretched out his hand.

"Ha-ha of course, of course." Mr. Wei agreed as he shook Min-jah's hand.

"So do you see anything in particular that you would like to have included in your inauguration celebration?" Mr. Wei asked as they continued to browse through the cakes.

"I'm actually not a fan of sweets but my late father loved this bakery." Min-jah says solemnly as he walks around the bakery.

"Ah, yes Chairman Lan. He was a much appreciated regular." Mr. Wei says with a sad smile. "I'm deeply saddened by his passing."

"Are all the cakes decorated by just one person?" Min-jah asks as he leans down to look at a strawberry decorated cake.

"Ah no, I have three pâtissiers employed." Mr. Wei says with an awkward cough.

"I see." Min-jah says uninterested as he moves on to the next set of counters.

"W-would you like a certain pâtissier?" Mr. Wei asks concerned.

Min-jah's eyes sparkle with excitement at the question.

"That would be perfect. I want the best one you have." Min-jah says excitedly. Mr. Wei's eyes grew wide as he began to understand.

"I see. You must have seen Joon decorating. I knew installing that window would be good for business." Mr. Wei says with excitement. "Although it's rare a male will watch him he usually only catches the eyes of the ladies who come in." he thought. "I understand completely, of course I'll let him know immediately." He says as he claps his hands together happily.

Min-jah smiles as he gives Mr. Wei another handshake to confirm his order.

"So his name is Joon?" Min-jah thinks as he and his bodyguards leave the bakery.

Mr. Wei's overly large smile immediately disappears as soon as the door to the bakery closes. He looks over at the window to see Joon decorating cupcakes. He lets out a sigh as he walks towards the kitchen.

"I just need to convince Joon to work on such a large order." Mr. Wei thinks as he walks through the kitchen door.

"Joon." he says as he lightly taps me on the shoulder.

Startled I rip my headphones out of my ears and take a step back and turn to look at him.

"Y-yes Mr. Wei." I stutter out.

"I know you don't usually work on large orders but the customer that was just here. He wants you to create something original for his celebration. And honestly without this order I won't be able to make this month's bills so if you could-" he rambled.

"Okay." I interrupted.

"What?" Mr. Wei said, surprised.

"I said okay, I'll do it." I said casually as I put one headphone back in my ear.

"Really?" Mr. Wei said with teary eyes.

"Now, now Mr. Wei, just because I have the extra time since I'm on break from school you aren't trying to keep me here? It's not like you actually need this order the bakery does just fine." I said mockingly.

Mr. Wei instantly goes serious "Really? And here I thought you actually cared. Fine." he says fake crying as he walks away.

I smile and shake my head as he walks out of the kitchen. Glancing back before he walks out he turns to look at Joon and smiles as he watches him pick up a bag of frosting.

"What a punk." Mr. Wei says with a smirk as the door closes.

I stood there looking at the undecorated cupcakes sitting on the counter in front of me. With a deep breath I put my headphones on pressed play and began to create my magic. When I decorate cakes it gives me a sense of ease and a sense that I'm normal in a way. Knowing that these cursed hands of mine that usually frighten people can create something that will bring a smile to the faces of those same people. Although I still have to keep a distance knowing my creations can make someone happy makes the loneliness seem almost worth it. I smile as I place the last pearl bead on the final cupcake.

"Yuki-ji, the cupcakes are ready." I say as I place the tweezers on the counter next to the container full of different colored beads.

"Okay!" shouts a voice from across the kitchen as she stands on her tip-toes to place a pan of hot fresh bread on a rack.

Yuki-ji is a petite young woman with curly red hair which she loves to wear in low pigtails despite being almost thirty years old. Although looking at her no one would say she looked a day over twenty years old. With an infectious happy go-lucky attitude and a smile as bright as the sun it's hard not to smile when she's around. Although she is my senior in this industry sometimes it's very hard to take her seriously because she can be very childish.

After stretching her arms out as far as she possibly physically could she takes a deep breath and stretches a little farther until the pan finally slides into place. With a triumphant smile Yuki-ji skips over happily with empty display pans for the cupcakes. I watched as she happily weaved through the kitchen staff making her way towards me. She places the pans on the counter with a large smile and one by one we both fill the pans.

"You won't believe the latest news about my precious baby." Yuki-ji begins looking at me for signs that I'm listening.

"And what would that be?" I asked, noticing she was staring at me.

With the brightest smile she begins to tell me all the gossip about the hottest new K-pop boy band. About how she swears the lead singer, Win Chu, is for sure going to be her husband. Of course she also said that about another lead singer until he was caught in a huge scandal and lost everything. I do not find this type of idle chatting entertaining even in the slightest. In fact, I find it tiresome and draining but seeing the way Yuki-ji lights up when we have these types of conversations; I feel like this little bit of suffering is worth it to see this blinding happiness.

As Yuki-ji continues to go on and on about Win Chu we fill the pans with the cupcakes. Filling the last pan her hand barely brushed against my arm. In that split second touch I saw it. I saw how Yuki-ji was going to die. It was dark, she was wearing a pink hoodie I've never seen her wear before. She is walking alone up an alley that only has one working street light when someone comes up behind her. Startled at first she feels relieved as she smiles like she knows who it was with her bright smile she turns around and continues walking. The person makes her turn around again and she looks down at the hands of the perpetrator. With the realization of what is about to happen Yuki-ji's carefree attitude fades away and is replaced with fear. Adrenaline begins to flood her body.

Pushing the person away from her she tries to run away but just as quickly as she came to this decision the man had grabbed her and started to drag her into the dark. Overwhelmed by all her fear, the determination to get free, the desperation for someone to walk by right at that moment I suddenly couldn't breathe. I could feel the coldness of a blade touching her skin as the man began to play with her fear. Gasping for breath I began to panic with a sudden sharp pain in my side I realized the man who was going to do this to Yuki-ji was going to drag it out as long as he possibly could. Yuki-ji lets out a blood curdling scream as the knife pierces her skin again.

Since the touch did not last longer than a few seconds the pain of the knife stabbing her brought me back to reality. Letting out a pained groan I collapsed clutching my side where the blade had pierced her skin. Panicked and still filled with the overwhelming sense of fear I began to hyperventilate. Instantly all my co-workers rushed to my side worried they were going to touch me I quickly held up an opened hand.

"I- I- I'm fine." I stuttered out breathlessly as I sat on the floor trying to control my breathing. I could hear Mr. Wei scolding Yuki-ji.

"What were you thinking?!" he shouted at her so loudly she flinched.

"You should know by now that you can't touch him!" He continued with a red face.

"I-I'm sorry, my hand just barely touched... I-I didn't-" Yuki-ji sobbed as she tried to explain to Mr. Wei that it was just an accident.

"I don't want to hear your excuses! Why aren't you wearing gloves anyway?! I need you to be more careful!" Mr. Wei continued scolding.

Do not misunderstand, no one here knows what happens when I touch someone. They all believe it's some sort of severe psychological condition that is triggered by physical touch. Why? Well because that is what I told them when I first started three years ago. I wanted to prevent anyone from having any reason to touch me to avoid having to explain anything.

I had become too relaxed and too comfortable again. I uneasily stood up and looked over at Mr. Wei still scolding Yuki-ji. On the verge of tears trying to hold it back by biting her lip Yuki-ji was standing there looking down at her feet. I knew I had to stop him before she actually started crying.

"Mr. Wei." I said as I braced myself against the counter. "It was just an accident, I'm fine really." I said through a forced smile.

Mr. Wei looked at me and reluctantly turned away from Yuki-ji still filled with anger. Yuki-ji looked over at me with tears in her eyes. I smiled at her as I threw up a little finger heart sign using my thumb and index finger. She cracked a small smile through her tears at my silly attempt to make her feel better. With the tension slowly diffusing, everyone began to relax and got back to work.

With my hand still firmly pressed against my side as I could still feel the pain I looked over to Yuki-ji who was smiling her bright and carefree smile again as she laughed with everyone. The forced smile I was wearing slowly faded away as I gripped my side harder. I began to wonder what kind of terrible person would want to snuff out that beautiful smile.

CHAPTER 2

Leaning against the wall outside the female workers locker room I was waiting for Yuki-ji to come out. I needed to come up with a plan to find out who was going to try to kill her. As I stood there pondering different ideas from straight out asking her to quietly stalking her until I found him, the door to the locker room creaked open.

"Yuki-ji" I said a little too quietly as she had not noticed me standing there.

"EEP!" she squeals loudly.

"Ah, sorry." I apologized as I took a step back.

"It's okay." she says with a laugh, "Why are you still here?"

"Ah. I just wanted to talk to you about today." I said awkwardly.

"Oh, about that I'm truly sorry. I wasn't aware your condition was that severe." she says apologetically as she fumbles with her ponytail.

"Ah." I say as I run my hand through my hair. I hate having to lie but I'd hate to lose her as a friend even more.

"It's pretty late let me walk you home." I say as I look back up at her.

Yuki-ji smiles "Okay!" she says happily.

"Great." I said with a smile as we both walked towards the alley exit.

A street light flickered on as we made our way up the hill towards her house. There was a piercing quietness between us that was borderline awkward. Feeling the weird tension between us growing I felt the need to break the awkwardness.

"Um-" we both said at the same time as we turned to face each other. We both chuckled as we quickly looked away from each other.

"You first." I said as I actually didn't have anything to say.

"Okay." Yuki-ji says with a smile, "You truly aren't mad at me right?"

"No, of course not. It was just an accident anyway." I confirmed.

"Phew! I was so scared!" she said with a sigh of relief. "I was worried I would be fired, or worse you would quit!"

"How is me quitting worse than you being fired?" I asked with a chuckle.

She smiled softly as she explained "Because I could easily find another job, but what about you? You are surrounded by people who are aware of your condition and are comfortable working with you. If you quit you would have to go through the whole process again. You would have to explain again, have to get to know another set of people who wouldn't understand at first." She chuckled and looked down as she continued. "Besides I really like watching you decorate the cakes. If you left I might not be able to watch you again." she smiles at me with that infectious smile of hers.

I couldn't help but nervously smile and blush at the sudden compliment. Suddenly it got very dark as we walked. I looked up to see that none of the street lights around us were working except one that was way ahead of us. I was instantly reminded why I offered to take her home. I began to look around us but it was hopelessly dark I couldn't see anything.

"Hey, are these street lights always off?" I asked as I continued to scan our surroundings.

"Ah, yeah I hate this part of my walk home." Yuki-ji says with a forced chuckle. "But the Oppa that lives next door always meets me at the street light up ahead, and walks me home when I'm out this late."

"Oppa?" I asked.

"Yeah, he noticed I come home late sometimes and told me how it was unsafe for a girl to be walking alone at night. So he meets me and walks me home sometimes." she explained happily, "He's so sweet."

"Hmm?" I thought to myself as she continued to babble about him.

"Oh look, there he is!" Yuki-ji says with a smile.

Out of the darkness a man walks out into the light being emitted by the street light. Wearing his black hair slicked back tan dress pants, a white buttoned up shirt that was rolled up to his elbows, and a pair of thick rimmed glasses he stood with his hands in his pockets. As we got closer I could tell right away he was not happy to see me. Yuki-ji runs towards the man standing in the light.

"Oppa!" she shouts as she takes off.

The man smiled gently as she got closer to him but instantly faded away once he noticed me following closely behind her.

"Yuki-ji, who is this?" he asked as I stepped into the glow of the light.

"This is Joon, we work together." Yuki-ji explained ecstatically.

"Hi." I greeted him.

"Hi." he said through a forced smile trying to hide his contempt. "Why are you suddenly walking Yuki-ji home?"

I chuckled as I looked at his icy cold black eyes that were piercing right through me. "We had a little incident at work today, just wanted to clear the air." I explained as I glared back at him.

"Ahaha..." Yuki-ji chuckled nervously, "Joon, thank you for walking me but I'll go the rest of the way with Oppa. See you at work tomorrow."

"Of course." I smiled, "See you tomorrow."

I waved goodbye as I turned to walk away. I could feel his intensely sharp stare like a dagger directed straight toward my back through the darkness. With a sudden twinge of pain in my side as I walked away I knew now without a doubt this has to be the man. The one who is going to kill Yuki-ji.

After that night I began walking Yuki-ji home every night after work and he was always waiting for her by the streetlight. I needed a way to get him away from her but work began to get extremely busy. I couldn't come up with a plan. With the inauguration party of a client drawing near I began to wonder when he would actually kill her. I haven't seen her once wear the pink hoodie like the one in my vision.

"EEEEKKKK!!!" Came a sudden squeal from the back of the kitchen.

Shocked, everyone jumped and stopped what they were doing and looked to see Yuki-ji looking at her phone with her mouth covered.

"Oh I'm sorry." She apologized with a gleeful smile.

"What is the matter?" I asked as I released my breath.

"You know Win Chu?" she began excitedly.

"How could I not?" I answered with a chuckle as I went back to work.

"Well he's going to be having a concert at the NXT Stadium in two months!" she squealed with excitement and began hopping around like a drugged up bunny.

"Oh." She stops suddenly, "They are also going to be giving away a limited edition hoodie only available to the first two hundred people that buy a ticket! Want to see a picture?" She says shoving her phone into my face so close I could smell the lotion on her hands.

"Oh, sorry." She says as she pulls back her hand from my face.

I snatched her phone out of her hand as soon as I caught a clear look at the hoodie. This is it, the hoodie Yuki-ji was wearing in my vision. I looked up from the phone to see a confused look on her face.

"I didn't know you were a fan." Yuki-ji says mockingly.

"Oh." I realized, "I'm not." I said as I handed back her phone.

"Oh." She said dejectedly as she reached out for her phone.

Yuki-ji grabbed her phone back shrugging off what I said and excitedly began to jump around again. Two months, is that all the time she had left? Fortunately that gave me plenty of time to come up with a plan to stop that man from killing her. For now I needed to focus on the party that was in a few days.

The day of the big event Mr. Wei walks into the kitchen looking more disheveled than he does on a regular day. Everyone was busy trying to complete all their daily morning tasks when Mr. Wei coughs to get everyone's attention.

"Listen up everyone," he began, "Now I know it's super early but today is a very important day so let's all stay focused and start preparing everything we are going to need." Mr. Wei looked around the kitchen to see all the staff looking at him with fake happy smiles. He chuckles as he looks around.

"Alright let's get started." He says with a smile as if all his worries just suddenly disappeared.

And with that the kitchen turned into a bustling organized mess. In the center were four people mixing the batter. Two people were measuring all the dry ingredients as two more were measuring the wet ones. On the left side of the kitchen one person was lining cupcake pans with tiny paper cups while another was pouring the batter into the molds. Further down the counter another person tapped out all the bubbles and placed the pans into the oven. Once the cupcakes were done they were placed on the cooling racks by Yuki-ji who would wheel them over to the pâtissiers' decorating stations where me and the two other pâtissiers were standing waiting.

As soon as the cupcakes were cool enough to be frosted, we started to get ready. Like a well-oiled machine all three of us began to move in a sequnized sequence. We rolled up our sleeves, tied on our aprons, put on black latex gloves, adjusted our chefs hats, grabbed an icing piping bag, a cupcake, and began the long day ahead of us. Like an assembly line we began decorating the cupcakes each with our own design. As we placed the finished cupcakes down, hands that appeared to come out of nowhere would grab the cupcakes and place them in boxes ready for transportation. Just as we finished one cooling rack Yuki-ji, with her usual bright smile, would bring another full rack our way and take the empty one to be filled again. I'm sure she actually enjoyed seeing the light drain out of our eyes every time. This train went on for hours with no end to be seen in sight. Just as my hands felt like they were going to fall off from decorating I placed the final touches on the last cake just hours before the event. With a loud cheer all the kitchen staff hollered as the last box of cupcakes was loaded into the delivery truck.

As if he could tell everyone was getting ready to finally relax Mr. Wei walks out of the bakery with a clipboard in his hands. Instantly everyone stopped celebrating already wary of what is about to be announced.

"Alright for six of you your day is not over yet." Mr. Wei said sternly.

Scattered groans ran through the crowd of staff members followed by grumbled complaints like a wave. Mr. Wei just scoffs at our blatant sign of disappointment.

"If I call your name you are required to attend the event and serve the guest on behalf of the bakery." Mr. Wei said loudly to drown out the complaints.

Knowing he would never send me to the actual event I began to slowly weave my way through the staff so I could be the first one to leave. As I was almost to the edge when I suddenly stopped because much to my surprise Mr. Wei just called out my name. I immediately whipped my head around to see everyone looking at me just as surprised. Nervously I chuckled and walked as fast as I could to Mr. Wei.

"Ahaha y-you're joking right?" I said through a very nervous chuckle.

"Nope." Mr. Wei brushed me off.

"But-" I protested.

"No 'buts' you were the requested pâtissier so you will be there. Now go home and get ready the event starts in four hours." He said coldly as he turned to walk back into the bakery.

Completely taken aback I was left there standing speechless as the rest of the staff slowly began to file away. I let out a heavy sigh as I unlocked the door to my apartment. I glanced at my watch as I took off my shoes and slipped on my house shoes. Still had over three hours until the event exhausted I decided to take a nap. I set an alarm as I dropped onto my bed taking a deep breath as I slipped off into a deep sleep.

I woke up being surrounded by darkness again, the floor has a thin layer of water as usual. My head splitting with an unbelievable headache, my leg aching as if it was broken, and a sharp intense pain in my ribs as if I had just been beaten. The only sound is the sound of my harsh breathing as I struggle to stand up. Unable to see anything I slowly reached out my hands to try to find something, anything in the dark that could help me figure out where I was. Walking along the seemingly never ending black wall, something begins to make my eyes sting. I reached up to wipe my eyes suddenly overwhelmed by a deep metallic scent that comes from blood. As I continue searching the wall a voice suddenly calls out my name from behind me. Startled, I quickly turned around.

"H-hello?" I stuttered out.

No one answered. My breathing began to echo in my ears as I slowly made my way toward the voice. As I started to get closer to what I thought was the origin I began to hear a dripping sound getting louder and louder. I started to limp toward the sound as I got closer I noticed there was a light at the end. Thinking I might actually be able to finally figure out where I am I limped as fast as I could. I stumbled and fell into the water as I reached the light. I laid in the water as I tried to keep my eyes open. I could feel all the strength leaving my body with all my might I reached up into the light. I desperately tried to hold my hand up. It felt like a thousand pounds but for some reason I felt like if I dropped my hand it would all be over.

"Joonie-ah!" an unfamiliar voice shouted.

Shocked by the sound of the voice saying my name all the remaining strength I had was sucked out and with a splash my hand fell into the water.

With the sound of my alarm ringing I suddenly jumped awake covered in a cold sweat with my arm stretched out as if it was reaching for something in the air. With a dejected sigh I dropped my arm. I dreamed it again, the exact moment of my death. I have had this dream several times now and it usually ended the same with me in a dark damp place dying alone. I rolled over and hit the alarm and got out of bed. As usual I have more questions than answers after the dream. Why was the ending different this time? Who was calling my name? And why did I feel so relieved to hear that voice?

Shaking the useless thoughts out of my head, I stood up and started to get ready for the event. I made my way to the bakery where the other five poor souls that were also chosen were waiting. Together we all loaded into the company van and set out for the venue.

"Alright guys all you have to do is smile as you pass out the cupcakes got it?" Mr. Wei announced as we all piled out of the van.

With no response Mr. Wei shouted through the van window "Hey did you guys catch that?!"

All of us still exhausted from the bustle of the morning gave a slight nod and a disgruntled wave as we walked toward the building. Mr. Wei rolls his eyes and huffs with annoyance as he drives away. Everyone begins to sleepily get ready by putting on the full white chef's coat and matching white gloves. Those with long hair had already pulled it back into a neat ponytail or bun to prevent hair from contaminating the cupcakes.

"Okay guys," I started softly, "we just have to make it through the next five hours and then we have the next three days off. Let's do this!"

Excited, everyone began to bustle through their tasks. As the cupcakes were being carefully placed on the displays in the hall I watched over and checked every little detail. With little to correct I began to make my way back into the kitchen when a waiter carrying red wine busted through the doors. Not expecting anyone to be there she jumped nervously as she bumped into me spilling wine on my gloves.

"Oh my goodness I am so sorry!" She exclaims as she tries to dry the wine.

"It's okay." I said as I looked at my stained gloves.

"I'm so sorry." She apologizes again as she turns around back into the kitchen.

I look at my hands and am reminded of my dream being covered in blood. I shook my head as I took off my gloves and walked into the kitchen.

"Does anyone have any extra gloves with them?" I asked.

Everyone looked up and shook their heads with a worried expression. I sighed as I put the gloves on the counter.

"That's okay." I said as I raised my hands up.

Hesitantly the staff went back to working on putting out the cupcakes. My hands were a little sticky from the wine I walked over to the closest sink to wash them.

"It will be fine." I thought "Just don't touch anyone. I can do that." I promised myself as I shook the water off my hands.

With the event happening in the VIP lounge of the hotel, we carefully started bringing up the tables full of cupcakes. The room had an all-around skyview that was absolutely breathtaking. In the center there were a dozen tables being set up with satin white tablecloths with gold trim. On the tables placed directly at the center was a small vase of beautiful white roses. The chairs that surrounded the tables were draped in a matching white cloth with a gold bow tied on the back. As the tables were being wheeled in, I directed each person to their expected position. With the last table finally in its place, the event was ready to begin.

A dozen reporters began to file in and take their place against the wall closest to the door. The room slowly came to life as the guests began to enter and find their seats. The room felt like a whole different world and despite the glamourous aura that was being emitted by everyone there I only felt uncomfortable. The room was filled with light music and chatter when a middle aged man wearing a grey suit with his hair slicked back to hide the grey strands walked in. Upon noticing him the wall of reports turned into a frenzy to get his picture. In response to the frenzy all the guests looked toward the door then there was the squeal of the microphone feedback that caught everyone's attention. Standing on the stage was a young man with a bright smile wearing a dark red suit with short curly hair to match.

"Thank you all for joining us," the young man said with a smile, "to start why don't everyone find their seats so we can begin."

With a silent agreement all the guests began to shuffle towards their seats. Annoyed, the middle aged man made his way to his seat by the stage. Once all the guests were seated the man on stage began speaking again.

"Once again I'd like to thank everyone who is here. For those of you who don't know me my name is Kim Byung-woo and my best friend is the only reason you are all here today. So without further delay, I'd like to introduce you to Chairman Lan Min-jah." he said with a warm smile as he motions toward the door.

With applause from all the guests the doors open as a tall young man strutted into the room. Wearing a black suit with his hands in the pockets of his pants his dark brown hair slicked up in an elegant way and a coy smirk that seemed to instantly melt the hearts of all the ladies, young and old alike, in the room. He makes his way towards the stage to join Kim Byung-woo waving and smiling at all the guests on his way. He shakes hands with Byung-woo on the stage who reciprocated with a smile and a pat on the shoulder as he walked off the stage. Min-jah walked up to the microphone and with a smile waited for the applause to quiet down.

"You guys flatter me." He said with a laugh. "I'm very humbled to be able to lead my father's company and I'm especially happy that all the Directors and stockholders believe in me. Of course I have huge shoes to fill, so don't be afraid to tell me if I'm not living up to your expectations. Although I hope no one will feel that way."

Scattered laughter filled the room as he continued with his speech. I couldn't help but stare at him as he confidently stood on the stage. The way his smile seemed so gentle as he looked into the sea of faces. The sound of his smooth deep voice resonated something deep inside of me like sweet honey to my ears. As he completed his speech the guests applauded and it was time for them to mingle amongst each other. Min-jah and Byung-woo began to make the rounds greeting all the guests. My eyes instinctively followed them around the room until they were standing in front of me. The middle aged man from earlier walked up to Min-jah and offered a handshake, which was promptly ignored.

With a slight chuckle as he retracted his hand he looked at Min-jah as if he just wanted to punch him.

"Is this the kind of attitude you choose to have towards your loving uncle? Hmm Min-jah?" He said through a smile as the reporters were watching.

"It's Chairman Lan, and if you wanted to be treated as a 'loving Uncle' then you should act like one Uncle." Min-jah said coldly as he stared at him.

I stood there watching as the tension between the two grew so thick you could cut it with a knife. Feeling the need to break up the atmosphere I grabbed two plates with cupcakes and offered them up.

"W-would you like a cupcake?" I asked nervously as I held up the plates.

They both looked at me making me feel even more nervous than I already was. Min-jah smiled warmly and took a plate putting me slightly at ease. I looked over at the middle aged man who was staring at me coldly as if I just killed his family dog or worse.

"I hate sweets." He scoffed as he walked away.

I groaned softly as the man walked away from us with his head lowered.

"Don't mind him, my Uncle is always like that." Min-jah said with a smile as he placed the cupcake down on the table.

"Ah, o-okay." I said.

"You are the patisserie, right?" Min-jah asks.

"Uh yeah, I am." I said softly.

"Mr. Joon, right?" Min-jah asks as he looks into my eyes.

I stared at him unable to say anything.

"W-what?" I finally managed to stutter out.

"Your name is Joon, right?" Min-jah asks again, looking at me for confirmation.

It was the voice from my dream, the one that calls out my name and leads me out of the darkness. The one that fills me with relief as if I had been longing for it. The one who finds me at the end of my dream. Who was this man to me?

CHAPTER 3

Confused Min-jah waves his hand in front of my face to get my attention. Realizing I had been staring I quickly looked away from him.

"Mmhm." I said quietly.

With a bright smile Min-jah extends his hand for a greeting.

"Nice to meet you. I instantly fell in love with your cakes, they are just breathtakingly beautiful." Min-jah says happily.

I looked at his hand nervously hiding my hands behind my back and tried to back away. Perplexed, he looked at me as I tried to escape from the situation. Holding my wrist tightly with one hand I bowed at him as I fled to the other side of the table. Min-jah grins as Joon runs away chuckling slightly as the cute expression of confusion that was on Joon's face becomes ingrained into his memory.

The party was in full swing when I began to feel light headed and nauseous. I stepped away from the tables full of cupcakes and braced myself against the back wall. Standing there with my eyes closed I took several deep breaths when a voice startled me from behind.

"Are you okay?" Min-jah asked concerned.

"Ah. I'm okay." I answered as I waved my hand at him.

With one more deep breath I stood straight up with a smile.

"See? I'm fine." I say as convincingly as I could.

"If you say so." he answered back unconvinced.

I flash a smile as I walk past him heading back to the tables when I accidently trip over my own feet. Instinctively Min-jah reaches out quickly and catches my wrist before I could even try to catch myself. I quickly look up at him as he holds my wrist above my coat. Sighing with relief he pulls me back into a standing position.

"I thought you said you were okay?" he says with a mocking chuckle.

"Ah ha," I chuckled back nervously, "Thank you."

Too busy fixing my coat I did not notice that my hair became tousled from almost falling. Staring at the pieces of hair out of place Min-jah reaches up and gently fixes Joon's hair. Joon stopped moving as his fingers gently glided across his forehead. With a gentle smile Min-jah lowers his hand only to have the smile fade away when he notices a single tear slide down Joon's cheek.

Before I could stop him Min-jah reached up and shifted the fringe of my bangs with his fingers. With the gentle strokes of his fingertips against my forehead I saw his death flash before my eyes. Standing in the middle of the room Min-jah was greeting various people when a reporter accidentally knocked over a glass of wine into the lap of a female guest causing a commotion. In the midst of the reporter trying to apologize, Min-jah was greeted by the chairman of another large company pulling his attention away from the angry guest. When a bullet shatters the window, going through Min-jah's skull, smashing the ice sculptor and finally coming to rest in the back wall. Before anyone could gather what was happening Min-jah's body collapsed on itself. Laying there in a pool of his own blood I begin to feel a sadness I have never felt before as the blood begins to seep out of his head. With a high pitched scream everyone in the room began to flee. I stood there staring at him when a single tear rolled down my face. With a gasp and a painful groan I grabbed my head in excruciating pain.

I looked to see Min-jah crouched down next to me concerned. He placed his hand on my shoulder and began rubbing as if to comfort me. Before the pain could even subside I heard a shriek from across the room followed by incoherent yelling. Behind him the chairman of JKL had just walked up to greet Min-jah.

Min-jah stood up to see what was happening upon seeing the chairman he instinctively greeted him with a smile. Suddenly terrified about what was about to happen I quickly reached out and grabbed his ankle and pulled as hard as I could. The window then suddenly shattered as Min-jah lost balance and began to fall, the bullet whizzed right past his head shattering the ice sculptor of the Lan business tower going into the wall.

Min-jah hit the floor flustered and angry he immediately looked back to see me grabbing his ankle as hard as I could. With a scream the guests began to panic and started to run out of the room.

After all the guests had run out of the room the only ones left in the room were me and Min-jah. Still squeezing his ankle, my finger slipped off his pants as he rolled over to sit up. I began to see another vision of Min-jah reaching his hand out to grab my shoulder when the gunman shot at him again hitting him in the chest. I gasped and let go of his ankle breathing heavily. I looked up to see Min-jah looking at me. Seeing me in a panic he started to reach up towards me. I immediately grabbed his forearm and pulled him closer to me ignoring the new pain in my chest. As I did another bullet whizzed by landing in the floor right next to us. We both looked at the bullet hole in the floor and scrambled to find shelter behind the closest table.

Panting as we finally made it to a table Min-jah cautiously peeked around the edge after several seconds. Another bullet then whizzed past him again landing in the floor. I quickly grabbed him and pulled him back to find blood trickling from a cut on his cheek. I ripped a piece of the table cloth and wrapped it around my finger. As I go to wipe the blood he firmly grabs my arm and stares at me with a glare cold enough to send chills through my whole body.

"W-what?" I stuttered out nervously.

Min-jah continues to stare at me coldly, not answering. Beginning to feel uncomfortable under his gaze I try to pull my arm back. Without blinking he pulled me close to him, I could feel the heat of his breath against my skin. Nervous there was nowhere else to look but into his deep brown eyes.

"Y-your bleeding." I managed to say breathlessly.

He slowly released his grip on my arm with those words and looked away with his injured cheek facing me. I took that to mean I had the okay to wipe the blood off his cheek. I slowly raised my hand towards his cheek and began carefully wiping the blood.

As I wiped the blood I began to wonder why I felt so sad as I watched the vision of his death. Why did I feel the need to save him so urgently? Why would I rather trade my own life for his? I only felt this way once before when I had first decided to use this curse for good.

"You're not trying to kill me right?" Min-jah finally says after several minutes.

"Why would I save you if I wanted you dead?" I answered slightly irritated at the question.

He sat silently as he didn't have an answer to my question. After several minutes he looks over towards the door and then back at me. Then with the sound of police sirens coming from a distance we sighed with relief.

"How did you know someone was going to try to shoot me if you weren't trying to kill me?" Min-jah asks with a serious tone as he looks at me. Before I could open my mouth a dozen bodyguards burst into the room instantly fanning out surrounding us.

"Min-jah!" Shouts a panicked voice from behind the bodyguards.

Pushing his way through Byung-woo smiles with relief as he sees Min-jah stand up.

"Oh thank god!" Byung-woo shouts out as he runs and hugs Min-jah.

I let out my breath quietly as I managed to dodge the question and silently slipped away from the now distracted Min-jah soothing the over dramatic crying Byung-woo. After finally managing to peel off, Byung-woo brushed off the dirt on his suit. With a chuckle as Byung-woo was being dragged out he turned around to find the patisserie was gone. Min-jah swirled around to scan the room quickly only to find he was nowhere in sight.

Having successfully snuck out of the main hall I made my way to the kitchen where I quickly changed my clothes. In a dark jacket, jeans with holes and my headphones snuggled deep inside my ears. I threw up the hood, shoved my hands into the coat pockets and looked down to hide my face. I then walked outside into the sea of first responders quickly and quietly I disappeared into the night.

Amidst all the chaos a dark midsized vehicle was parked off in the distance. From the back seat a cell phone rang once and was then answered immediately.

"Sorry sir.." came a man's gravely voice through the phone.

Irritated he hastily hung up the phone and nodded toward the driver who put the vehicle in motion. Having taken off in a hurry the driver just barely missed a young man wearing dark clothes. Grumbling under his breath while looking out the window he clenches the phone tightly out of frustration as his plan had failed.

I quickly jumped out of the way as a dark vehicle came launching towards me. As the back of the vehicle passed I briefly saw the angry face of the man that was introduced as the Chairman's uncle with the light from his phone. I shook my head as I watched the vehicle disappear.

With lights flashing and sirens still blaring, Min-jah makes his way through the crowd when a scruffy middle-aged man walks up to him.

"Hello I'm detective Ma," the scruffy man introduced as he flashed his badge, "you are Chairman Lan correct?"

"Ah yes I am." Min-jah answered as he lifted his hand to tell his bodyguards to stop.

"Perfect. I'd like to get your statement about what happened here tonight." Detective Ma says as he motions to a quieter area.

"Of course." Min-jah agrees as they both walk to the agreed upon area.

Min-jah then tells the detective everything he remembered. From the list of names of everyone who was there to how he fell just before he was shot at. Attentively listening Detective Ma wrote down everything that he said.

"Now how did you trip?" Detective Ma asks without looking up from his notes.

"Oh a staff member tripped me." Min-jah says, trying to see what notes he was making.

"And do you know this person?" Detective Ma asks while writing more notes.

"He came with the staff from the bakery we hired. I think he said his name was Joon?" Min-jah says nonchalantly.

Detective Ma pauses as soon as he hears the name. Min-jah notices his reaction to the mention of Joon's name and quizzically raises his eyebrow. With a click of his tongue Min-jah pulls out his business card and hands it to Detective Ma.

"If you have any other questions just call me." Min-jah says as he hands over his card.

"O-oh." Detective Ma says as he is pulled back from his thoughts and grabs the card.

"Byung-woo." Min-jah says after walking away from the detective.

"Yes." Byung-woo answers as he suddenly appears at his side.

"The patisserie named Joon gather all the information you can about him." Min-jah commands as he gets into the backseat of his company car.

With a nod as the driver closes the door Byung-woo immediately makes a call and walks away.

"First name Joon, works at Crowns Bakery on 14th street." Byung-woo says quickly and then instantly hangs up.

I could still hear the echo of the sirens as I walked down the dimly lit street towards my home. I let out an audible sigh as I tugged my hood tighter around my face. With four soft beeps followed by a louder click I opened my door to my already lit home. I closed the door as I tossed my bag and shuffled out of my shoes.

The little tune let me know my door had locked itself. I began to strip off the layers of clothing leaving a trail as I walked to my bed. I grabbed the navy blue pajama pants I had draped across my office chair and slipped them on. I crawled into bed with a smile suddenly very happy I had the next three days off. With a sigh of relief I hugged Mr. Snuggles and drifted off to sleep.

I woke in a dream I've never had before. There was a cool breeze blowing against me as if trying to tell me which way to go. A little curious I went with the flow of the wind showing me around places I have been to before. When I was suddenly walking down an unfamiliar street. I stopped in my tracks to try to find where I was when the wind started to blow harder pushing me forward against my will. The wind stopped blowing as soon as I was in front of a very strange looking store. The sign hanging above the door simply read MAMA TOOKIE. Looking through the large store window, it looked like the place was full of shelves lined with handmade pots and bowls. The door creaked loudly as I pushed it in. Once inside I saw wooden barrels that looked to be filled with some sort of clear stones or crystals.

"Welcome seer of death," came a crackly voice from the back of the store, "remember where I am located for you will need me soon."

Suddenly an address flashed before me, 33-16 Doungson. I heard a soft cackle of a laugh followed by a loud knocking on my door which jolted me awake. I groaned as I shielded my eyes from the sunlight that was leaking from the window. I picked up my phone to see it was only 7AM when another loud knock came from my door. Annoyed at how early and loud this person was, I rolled out of bed.

"Alright, alright." I groaned through a yawn.

I swung open my door squinting at the highly un-welcomed guest. As soon as I opened my door the uninvited invited himself and pushed right past me.

"Ah yes come right in officer Ma." I said sarcastically as I closed the door behind him.

As my eyes adjusted to the light, I saw a scruffy man who looked like even a full week of sleep wouldn't get rid of the dark circles around his eyes. He was wearing a frown as I walked past him and laid back down on the bed covering my face with my arm.

"What happened last night?" He bellowed loudly as if I wouldn't be able to hear him at a regular shout.

"I'm sure you heard from everyone who was there already." I said softly as I snuggled deeper into my bed.

"Why did you trip Chairman Lan just seconds before the shot?" He asked annoyed.

"Because tripping a Chernobyl sounded like fun." I answered with a sigh as I knew I wasn't going to be able to fall back asleep.

"You know what!" He pointed at me, "You have been involved in 64 of my cases this year alone there's no way for it to be just coincidence anymore." He stated.

I looked up at him from under my elbow and sighed softly as I sat up.

"You know these surprise morning visits from you *officer* are thrilling but I have not nor do I plan on doing anything illegal so if you could..." I said sarcastically as I motioned towards the door and laid back down.

"It's Detective." He growled before he walked out and slammed the door.

"Why is it always him?" I grumbled, "It's like they only have one detective in the whole precinct."

The water knobs turned with a squeak as the water was shut off. Stepping out of the shower wearing nothing but a towel Min-jah wipes the water off the mirror to show the small cut he received as a souvenir from last night's debacle. He walks out of the bathroom into a giant walk-in closet with suits and matching shoes lining the walls. In the center is a dresser that has a glass top half that shows an endless number of different colored and style neckties. The other half displayed his large selection of expensive watches. Unsatisfied with the solid black tie the maid picked out Min-jah thumbed through the ties and settled on a dark navy blue one that had black diamond shapes on it.

Min-jah tightened his tie and with one more quick look in the full body mirror he smiled as he admired his reflection. A soft knocking comes from the bedroom door as the housekeeper slowly opens it.

"It's time to go Sir." The soft spoken housekeeper said with her head down.

Acknowledging with a nod he walks past the housekeeper swiftly who immediately closes the door behind him. Waiting outside next to the back passenger door which was already opened was his driver. Without missing a beat Min-jah immediately slipped into the vehicle and with a soft thud the door closed behind him.

Upon arriving at the Lan Company business tower Min-jah was greeted by a whole fleet of bodyguards. Twenty guards all together ten on each side making a path straight to the door. The driver instantly got out and rushed to open the door for him. Min-jah gets out and notices his uncle staring at the welcoming party Min-jah confidently walks inside out of spite. Annoyed, he rolled his eyes and scoffed at Min-jah as he walked inside.

Min-jah is closely followed by the twenty guards and various employees as he walks through the lobby. Without looking up as soon as Min-jah walked up to the security gates all ten doors automatically opened. Byung-woo immediately slipped up right behind Min-jah as soon as he stepped through the security gates. They both stepped into the elevator leaving behind the crowd of bodyguards and employees. Byung-woo hit the button for the 28th floor and the doors closed as the elevator silently started to rise.

The doors opened with a loud ding as it reached its destination. The floor had multiple sets of cubicles in bunches of four. There was a full glass wall, with white blinds that reached from the ceiling to the floor, that separated a large meeting room from the cubicles. Nodding at the random employees who bowed as they passed. They walked toward The Chairman's office which was located at the far end of the floor. Once inside the room opens up to ceiling to floor windows with dark colored blinds designed to block out the sunlight once closed.

To the left a small handcrafted wooden table that has a dark blue resin going through the center like a river is placed in the middle of two black leather couches with a matching single seater at the head of the table. On the right was a large wooden desk with piles of binders that needed to be approved and a name plaque that read Chairman Lan Min-jah. While glancing around the office Min-jah couldn't help but feel a little sad as just two weeks ago his father was the one sitting at that desk. Byung-woo immediately started to debrief Min-jah on the information he had found.

"So his name is Park-Chul Joon, he's 23 years of age, he has no parents..." Byung-woo says quickly.

"Are they dead?" Min-jah interrupts.

"Not that I found, they gave him up at the age of three to an orphanage reason unknown, after that they dissapeared without a trace. He was picked by a few families but they always brought him back after a few days. The longest family to house him was for a month he was brought back only a few days before the whole family was brutally murdered, after that he was never chosen again." He explained "he spent the rest of his childhood at the orphanage until he turned 18 when they kicked him out. Had a few run-ins with the law before turning 19 and then turned it around when he got the job at Crown's been working there ever since."

"How does that detective from last night know him?" Min-jah asks curiously.

"Interestingly Park-Chul Joon seems to be connected to quite a few of those Detective's open cases." Byung-woo says astonished.

"Connected how?" Min-jah asks, suddenly interested.

"Well, he is either a witness or directly involved. He has saved four people from drowning, three from committing self-harm, and 42 people from being attacked." Byung-woo says shocked as if he doesn't even believe what he is saying.

"What?!" Min-jah exclaimed wide eyed.

"Yeah, according to the reports he *just happens* to be passing by when the people are about to be attacked and he jumps in between and fights with the attacker long enough for the police to show up." Byung-woo continues "Strangely the police always receive an anonymous tip giving the exact location of where the person is going to get attacked minutes before anyone actually calls it in."

Min-jah leans back in his chair completely baffled at what he was told. He looks up at Byung-woo who also seems baffled and wondering who Park-Chul Joon was.

"Does he have any connection with the people he saved?" Min-jah asked, confused as he tried to put the pieces together in his head.

"Uh" Byung-woo hesitates as he scrolls through all the reports. "No, all the victims state that they have never seen nor have they met him before." He says puzzled.

Min-jah rapidly taps the top of his desk with his index finger as he continues to pounder their conversation. With his curiosity reaching the limit in a few short seconds he burst out of his chair and started pacing.

"What kind of person puts themselves in danger to save a complete stranger and then just keeps doing it?" Min-jah says angrily as he paces. "Doesn't he realize how dangerous that is?"

Min-jah continues pacing and mumbling to himself when he suddenly realizes Byung-woo is staring at him. With a nervous chuckle he stops pacing and sits down at the desk where he starts rapidly bouncing his leg instead. Slightly concerned Byung-woo continued with his morning briefing apprehensively.

"Why did you need this information?" Byung-woo asks for confirmation.

Min-jah nods and waves his hand at him aggressively as if telling him to move on.

"Um okay? Anyways... Because he seems to suspiciously show up at the right moment Detective Ma is convinced he has some sort of hero complex or is the mastermind behind all the attacks. So he is fixated on trying to catch him but seems more like a baseless accusation." Byung-woo says with a disagreeable tone. "To me he doesn't actually like to be acknowledged, he has been awarded the outstanding citizenship award four years in a row now and declined them every time. Seems like the detective just doesn't like him."

Min-jah sits back in his chair as he gazes out the window. Thinking to himself that there's no way this could be a simple coincidence. He suddenly recalls how desperately Joon clung onto his ankle making him fall just seconds before the first bullet. How he pulled him closer to avoid the second one as if he somehow already knew it was coming. Min-jah clicks his tongue in confusion, unable to make any sense about last night's events.

He leans on the desk knocking a pile of binders onto the floor. Irritated at himself he goes to pick them up.

"That's right," he thinks, "I'll just work so I won't think about it."

Having silently made up his mind Min-jah shoos Byung-woo away so he can get to work.

CHAPTER 4

Having signed binder after binder his hand felt like it was going to go numb. Min-jah rubs the bridge of his nose with his thumb as Byung-woo walks in with more binders and a white mug with a giant red heart on it filled with tea. Min-jah groans loudly showing his obvious contempt for the workload as Byung-woo walks towards him with a chuckle.

"Nothing urgent you can sign all these tomorrow morning." Byung-woo reassures him as he hands Min-jah the tea and places the stack down. "I'll tell them to get the car ready."

With a satisfied sigh Min-jah agrees and happily drinks the tea. Ready to go Min-jah packs up and leaves the office saying goodbye to the few employees that were still there. On the ride home Min-jah started to feel very sleepy. He tried to fight the urge to sleep ultimately losing by leaning his head against the car window he drifted off to sleep.

Woken up by the sound of someone calling his name Min-jah found himself standing in the middle of a dark street. Looking around he began to see a person running towards him quickly. Confused he lifted his hands up in a defensive position ready to strike. As the person running toward him got closer he recognized the person's face.

"What?" he asks as Joon's face becomes clearer.

"Follow me." Joon answers breathlessly and holds out his hand.

"Um okay?" he says, very confused but takes his hand anyways.

Walking hand in hand he leads him through various streets until they suddenly stop in front of a store. Joon let go of his hand and with a smile nodded toward the store. Min-jah looks up to see a sign that read MAMA

TOOKIE in large letters. He gulps as he reaches for the door handle. He slowly peeks inside to see the store was completely empty except for a counter in the far back. There was nothing, not even trash on the floor. Only more confused he pushed the door all the way open and walked inside.

Looking around something shiny on the back counter caught his attention. He slowly walked closer until he could see it was a simple gold necklace with a dark blue colored crystal being the only thing on the counter. Min-jah got an inexplicably strange feeling wash over him as if that necklace was somehow very important to him. Almost instinctively he goes to reach for it when a sudden booming voice startles him.

"The stronger the bond the darker the color. The darker the color the harder to break the bond." A strange crackly voice repeated over and over.

Min-jah frantically began to search for where the voice was coming from but it echoed over and over surrounding him as the words repeated. Being overwhelmed Min-jah covers his ears and closes his eyes tightly in an attempt to drown out the voice.

He is suddenly jolted awake by his driver, who also flinches, calling his name. Still shaken by the strange dream Min-jah doesn't realize he was sitting in his driveway for several seconds. After realizing where he was Min-jah gets out of the car and apologizes for scaring the driver. Feeling a little faint Min-jah braces himself against the car hood as he shakes his head. Thinking it was nothing more than just exhaustion Min-jah brushes it off wanting to go inside so he can sleep.

Standing on the opposite side of the kitchen Yuki-ji stares as Joon effortlessly makes buttercream flowers on top of a dozen cupcakes. She lets out a soft sigh as a beautiful smile spreads across the wonderful masterpiece that was his face. From the way he effortlessly manipulates the frosting to do his every command to lightly brushing his bottom lip while thinking to how he scrunches his nose when he laughs, she falls more in love. Content watching she completely forgets where she is and what she's actually supposed to be doing.

"Yuki-ji? YUKI-JI!!" hollers a voice from a nearby waiter named Chang.

"W-what?!" she hollers back startled.

"I need my order." he answers back suspiciously.

"R-right!" Yuki-ji says as she scrambles to put the last of the order together.

Letting out a sigh as Chang finally walks away with his order she looks back over to the pâtissier's station to see he is gone. Disappointed she looks down and continues to put orders together.

Three weeks had suddenly flown by in the blink of an eye. Between all the approvals, board meetings, and inspections of all the hotels, restaurants, and hospitals Min-jah barely had time to breath. While preparing for another meeting in his office Min-jah is interrupted by the intrusively loud Byung-woo.

"Ello," Byung-woo says in a poorly executed English accent. "Time for lunch!" He smiles as he flashes two sandwiches and a carrier with two drinks.

"Finally," Min-jah says as he tosses the papers in his hands, "I'm starving!"

Byung-woo excitedly enters the office and brings over their lunch. Putting all working matters aside they joyfully enjoy their lunch together. Although Byung-woo is three years older than Min-jah, they have always been inseparable. He was the son of the adored housekeeper for the Lan's estate. Despite her untimely passing when Byung-woo was in his last year of high school. And the sudden death of Min-jah's own mother less than a year later. The two only became closer throughout the years regardless of the countless objections from Min-jah's father.

Byung-woo takes a sip of his drink looking at Min-jah who was struggling to swallow his food.

"Are you okay?" Byung-woo asks with his eyebrow raised as he sips his drink.

"Yeah." Min-jah coughs and winces as he forces the food down. "Throat has just been a little sore lately."

"Do you want to go to the doctor?" Byung-woo asks quizzitivley.

"No I'm sure it's nothing, I'm fine." Min-jah says blowing off the pain.

Byung-woo stares at Min-jah as he pushes through the pain and continues to eat.

Looking up from placing a cheesecake in the display case to notice several customers whispering and looking out the window very worrisome. I glance outside and see Detective Ma leaning against his old beat up clunker. Looking like he hasn't had a decient nights sleep in over three months he glances over with a toothpick hanging out of his mouth like an old time gangster. With an annoyed sigh I swiftly untie my apron and go outside.

"You have been watching me for weeks, don't you have *actual* criminals to catch or is your badge just for show?" I say as I cross the street towards him.

"Ha I almost forgot how funny you are." He barks back with a fake laugh.

"Great and I almost forgot how ugly you are," I said unamused, "you are scaring the customers so unless you have a legitimate reason for being here, I'm going to have to ask you to please leave."

"I'm not going anywhere until I can place you in cuffs." He growled at me.

"Okay then." I replied with a shrug as I walked back to the bakery.

The door dings as I walk through Mr. Wei now aware of the disturbance comes out of the back office.

"What's going on?" He asks as he looks outside.

"Oh just some smelly homeless man causing a scene, I asked him to leave but he doesn't want to so I'm going to call the police." I say with a slight smile.

"Ok good," Mr. Wei says, "let's get this taken care of quickly."

I picked up the bakery phone smiled and waved at Detective Ma through the window as I dialed 119. Annoyed he mocked me by forcing a smile and waving back at me, I couldn't help but laugh.

"Yes hello?" I said as the line was picked up, "Yeah I'd like to report a suspicious and highly angry homeless man outside Crown's Bakery."

Ten minutes go by when a police vehicle pulls up beside Detective Ma. A few heated words, hand tossing, and finger pointing towards the bakery later Detective Ma is forced to leave by the patrol officer. He angrily looks toward the bakery where I am standing looking at him through the window along with many customers. I could not resist and gave him a little smile and a wave goodbye as he opened his car door. I'm sure if this was a cartoon his head would have exploded from anger at that moment.

I laughed silently as I made my way back into the kitchen. After a full day of baking, cooling, and decorating cake after cake it was finally time to go home. I looked around the kitchen one last time to make sure everything was put away and spotless. Satisfied, I turned off the lights. I zipped up my jacket as I walked out of the locker rooms to find Yuki-ji waiting for me.

"Let's go." I said with a smile.

With the day getting closer I decided to stick to Yuki-ji's side like glue so I could protect her. We have made it a habit to wait for each other after work when we are both working late. I had even started walking her all the way to her building despite her neighbor showing up. I was hoping with my presence I could scare him off or at least make it that much harder for him. I waved goodbye to Yuki-ji as she unlocked her apartment door. I waited for her to be safely inside before turning around to leave.

It was unusually dark as I made my way back down the hill to the bus stop. I got this strange sensation like someone was watching me. Unless the neighbor was craftier than I had anticipated as I saw him go into his apartment, it had to be someone else. I started walking faster to shorten the length of time I was in between streetlights. With the bus rounding around the corner I decided to start running. Immediately I heard the thud of footsteps besides my own coming up behind me. I started to run even faster and the footsteps picked up their pace as well. The bus pulled into the stop, I flew inside the second the doors opened. I swiped my wallet with a beep as I quickly made my way to the first available seat.

I stared at the door waiting for the person to get on when the doors closed and the bus began to move. I quickly got up and rushed to the back of the bus to try to see the person who was following me. As the bus drove away all I saw was a silhouette of the person as they stepped out of the dark and into the poorly lit bus stop I caught the slight shimmer off something metallic as they watched the back of the bus. Based solely on the approximate height of the silhouette and the presence of what appeared to be a knife I concluded that it had to be the neighbor. Slightly relieved I had become the new target. Confident I could stop him, I settled into the bus stop for the ride home.

Min-jah having fought his way through yet another series of constant coughing he rubs his throat and winces at the pain. Not letting this apparent cold get in the way of his work he opted out of going to the doctor yet again. He did, however, start taking cold medicine but to no avail as he was only getting worse. Seating at the desk looking over a proposal he suddenly has a craving for something sweet. Byung-woo comes in with a glass of tea looking concerned as he could hear Min-jah's coughing through the door.

"Perhaps you should go in for a checkup." Byung-woo suggests as he hands Min-jah the tea.

"I don't have the time," he coughs, "I need to finish reading all these proposals before this afternoon's board meeting."

"I could help you go through them." Byung-woo offers as he picks up one of the binders.

"Don't be silly," Min-jah says as he takes the binder, "You know that only the CEO can read these."

"Right..." Byung-woo says disheartedly.

Min-jah lets out a huge sigh as he rubs between his eyes and shrinks down into his chair. The chair slowly spins in a circle as Min-jah continues to rub his eyes.

"Ah you know what, I want some cake." Min-jah says perking up as he quickly turns to face Byung-woo.

"So you have time to leave the office for cake but not to go to the doctor?" Byung-woo asked him with a raised eyebrow.

"I can afford cake. I can't afford to be sick." Min-jah smiles brightly as he grabs his coat.

Shaking his head as he admits defeat, Byung-woo follows Min-jah out the door with a smile. Looking down from the 24th floor from the corner office watching as Min-jah and Byung-woo leave was Lan Hong-gi, Min-jah's uncle. The chief Director of the Crest, a large hotel chain under the Lan's, Hong-gi grumbled with anger as he watched. He staggered back to his desk to sit down as his cell phone rings.

"Did you find him?" Hong-gi asks immediately.

"Yes," answered the voice on the phone, "He works at Crown's Bakery as a pâtissier."

"Got it." he answered and then hung up the phone.

Byung-woo and Min-jah walk into the bakery laughing and shoving each other. Ignoring the fact that they are both adults and wearing suits they continued to mess around as they sat down in the cafe section. As a waitress brings them menus Min-jah glances at the large window into the kitchen. Byung-woo catches his attention as he sits down at the table. Min-jah quickly looks away as they continue to goof around.

I walked back to my station after helping Yuki-ji clean up the flour she had dropped. I glanced up as something moving quickly caught my attention. Much to my surprise it was Lan Min-jah and Kim Byung-woo acting like high schoolers. I smiled as I watched them, my smile faded away as I noticed something seemed strange.

Despite his large smile his color seemed paler then that night. As he was laughing loudly he suddenly started coughing violently which quickly put an end to the fun they were having. Min-jah raised his hand, stopping Byung-woo from coming over as his coughing fit came to an end.

"Don't need you catching whatever I have." Min-jah coughed out "I'm fine honestly."

Not convinced Byung-woo hesitantly sat back down. They then quietly looked over the menu.

"What's the house surprise?" Min-jah asks a passing waiter.

"Oh uh, you select a patisserie and they create a one of a kind dessert for you." The waiter explained with a smile.

"Perfect I'll order this." Min-jah says with a smile.

"And for you sir?" The waiter asks, turning to Byung-woo.

"I'll just have a slice of cheesecake." Byung-woo answers as he closes his menu.

The waiter grabbed both menus and went to walk away when with a gasp he quickly turned back around.

"Who would you like to create your dessert?" He quickly asks.

Min-jah cracks a large smile as the waiter waits for his answer. The large kitchen doors swing open with a clang as the waiter announces the order.

"I need a house surprise!" He shouts.

Fei, Deok-su, and I look up from our stations desperately wanting to be the one chosen. With a house surprise the patisserie has complete freedom to make whatever he desires. The waiter can see the look of anticipation on their faces as he was about to announce who got the order.

"It's an order for..." he trails off to build the tension "Joon!" He laughs.

The other two groan loudly in obvious disappointment as they go back to decorating cupcakes. I smile as I place the piping bag down on the counter.

"Who's the customer Chang?" I ask happily.

He points out the window towards the table where Min-jah and Byung-woo were sitting. I stared as Min-jah slowly sipped some cold water wincing as he swallowed. Knowing exactly what to make I began to hand out directions.

"Chang," I started, "Bring me two glazed doughnuts and some doughnut holes from the floor. Yuki-ji I'll need your help."

Yuki-ji popped her head up over the counter with a smile and a salute from Chang I tied my apron and walked to the stove. In a medium frying pan I began to melt two tablespoons of butter. Once the butter was completely melted and bubbling lightly I tossed the glazed doughnuts in. Cooking them on each side until the glaze was perfectly caramelized.

I quickly transferred them to a paper towel where Yuki-ji instantly started blotting them with a paper towel. I drop the fried doughnuts, half a cup of cream, and one and a half cup of whole milk into a blender. Once blended I poured the mixture into a sauce pan. Where it's heated over medium heat stirring occasionally until it starts to simmer. I then began my place setting.

I poured the soup-like mixture into a large brimmed bowl. I grabbed a blow torch and lightly heated the side of a doughnut hole and carefully placed four of them in a row on the edge of the bowl. Taking a step back I softly rubbed my bottom lip realizing it was missing something. I grabbed a sifter and sprinkled a little nutmeg lightly on the top and added a small mint leaf right in the center. I nodded toward Chang to let him know it was done. As he came over I slipped a small folded piece of paper next to the bowl unnoticed.

Chang places a piece of cheesecake and the 'house surprise' down on the table. Confused as to why he was just served soup at a bakery, Min-jah stops the waiter from walking away.

"May I ask what this is?" Min-jah says pointing towards the bowl.

Chang smiles as he begins to explain "Our pâtissier noticed you might have a cold so he made you what is traditionally called doughnut soup. It's warm and is said to soothe sore throats. Please enjoy your meal."

Min-jah couldn't help but have a silly grin on his face as he slowly stuck his spoon into the soup. Hesitantly he brings the spoonful to his mouth and is pleasantly surprised as the creamy mixture goes down easily. He smiles as he continues to eat. Once he was finished he sighed satisfied and placed the spoon down next to the bowl. He then notices a small piece of paper that is folded next to the bowl. Glancing up to find Byung-woo had gotten up to pay the bill, he quickly grabbed the paper and unfolded it.

Hey, you look very pale. Are you feeling okay? If not you should go see a doctor. I have tomorrow off if you are scared of doctors or something I could go with you If you want? +82 97 4351 x990

Min-jah glances up to see Joon completely focused on decorating he sweetly smiles as he looks away. Byung-woo walks up, catching his attention Min-jah quickly pulls out ₩10,000 and places it on the table. After finishing the cake I took out my headphones and looked up noticing that they had already left. I stood there wondering if he was feeling any better after eating. I began to clean up my station as I didn't have to walk Yuki-ji home tonight. I was excited to be getting off early.

I was putting my apron in my locker after changing when I noticed I had a notification on my phone. I placed my finger on the home button which automatically unlocked my phone. I saw a message from an unknown number.

I'm definitely not scared of doctors but I can play hooky tomorrow if you still want to go?

I smiled and then instantly frowned as I began typing back. I quickly hung up my apron and closed my locker as I hit the send button.

So does that mean you are actually sick?

My phone dinged as I waved goodbye to the night shift and walked out the door. Pausing to take my thumbs out of my gloves I started to walk to the bus stop.

Well... ☺

I shook my head as I stepped onto the bus and paid the fare. I sat down in the closest seat and wrote him back.

How long have you been feeling sick?

A little over two weeks... maybe?

Two weeks?? And you haven't gone to the doctor?

😬

Why wait until tomorrow you need to go now!

I can't today, can't slip away.

But you can tomorrow?

That's right.

You are going first thing?

Yep.

Okay.

Then I'll see you tomorrow morning.

I quickly sent him my address and then got off the bus. I couldn't help but be curious about him after his voice showed up in my dream. I felt pretty bad that I am only getting close to him to satisfy my own curiosity. Putting my gloves back on properly I started to walk home.

Min-jah was looking down at his phone smiling like a fool when Byung-woo walked in with his nightly tea. Not noticing him until he places the cup down Min-jah suddenly puts his phone down.

"What are you smiling at?" Byung-woo asks as he sits down.

"Oh… nothing." he answers with a smile as he sips the tea.

Suddenly motivated Min-jah stands up and stretches making his back pop.

"Bring me everything that needs to be approved first thing tomorrow morning." Min-jah says with a bright smile.

"Umm okay?" Byung-woo answers confusedly as he does as he was asked.

Min-jah sits back down and continues to work while drinking the tea.

The next morning Byung-woo comes into the office and starts on his morning routine. He greets all the secretaries and employees reminding them of any important events that are coming up. He starts making coffee, selecting a few cookies to compliment it. He then walks toward the office with a tray that has the coffee and cookies. He lightly knocks on the door before he slowly opens it.

"Good-" he stops short as Min-jah was not in his office.

Confused, he looks back at the other employees who were working busily.

"Where is he?" Byung-woo asks with a nervous chuckle.

All the employees stopped and stared unable to answer the question.

"Well… FIND HIM?!" Byung-woo shouts in frustration making the employees scurry into action.

I walk outside to see Min-jah standing next to his black sports car checking his teeth in his side mirror while he waits. He smoothes the creases out of his burgundy suit and leans back against the driver door looking like a cool rich guy that anyone could fall in love with. I pulled up my hood and slipped my hands into my pockets while I walked down the stairs. Min-jah looks around when he notices me walking towards him and begins to smile. Seeing the way his face lit up made me feel even more guilty but I couldn't help but smile too.

CHAPTER 5

Knowing that if he waited for the housemaid to wake him he would have to go to work. Min-jah sets his alarm for 6AM with a smile as he snuggles into bed. Starting her day off like any other the maid made her way to the main bedroom right before 7AM.

"Time to-" she cuts off as she finds the bedroom empty. "-get up." she continues softly.

Woken up by the sound of an incoming text message I drowsily hit the home button to check the time. I groaned softly as it was only 7:30AM. I pulled the covers over my head and started to snuggle deeper into my bed. Shocked, I grabbed my phone and hit the home button again to realize the message was from Min-jah.

Mission success. I am on my way.

I quickly jumped out of bed and ran into the bathroom, turning on the water. I scrambled to find clean clothes as I hadn't done laundry yet. I found a pair of faded blue jeans that were a little distressed at the knees. Looking like I bought them that way I quickly pulled them on. The only shirt I could find was a white v-neck that I usually wore under my chef's jacket. My phone dings again as I pull the shirt on over my head. I grabbed a pair of mismatched socks out of my top drawer and started towel drying my hair as I checked my phone.

Are you awake? I'm outside.

I violently dried my hair the best I could with the towel, grabbed my jacket off the back of my office chair, and slipped on a pair of white sneakers. I walked outside brushing my fingers through my wet hair to smooth it out the best I could. I began to put on my jacket as I noticed Min-jah wearing a burgundy colored suit leaning against a black sports car. My heart skipped a beat as I glanced down at him standing there waiting for me. Suddenly self-conscious, I pulled my hood up to hide my face as I made my way down the stairs.

Min-jah smiled a sweet smile as I walked up to him making me smile too. We awkwardly stood there for a few seconds before we remembered why we were meeting up to begin with.

"A-are you ready?" I asked nervously.

"Ah y-yeah!" Min-jah chuckles as he unlocks the car.

"Great, let's go." I said with a deep breath as I walked around the car.

The interior was just as luxurious as the outside. The seats were made of black leather with red enhancements. The dash board was solid black and the buttons on the radio could only be seen because they lit up red once the car was on. From the inside I couldn't hear the engine but if I touched the car I could feel it's beautiful purr coursing through me. Excited, I looked over at Min-jah with a huge smile who was looking back at me and started laughing as he drove away.

Min-jah parks the car as close as he could to the front doors of the hospital. I frowned as the ride was suddenly already over. Min-jah grabbed his phone as it started to ring for the seventh time. He silenced the ringing and tossed his phone into the cup holder.

"Don't worry, we have all day." Min-jah says with a smile as he opens the door.

I ran my hand across the leather seats one more time as I got out of the car. I blew on my hands as they were a little cold and suddenly realized I forgot to grab my gloves. I quickly shoved them into my jacket pockets. We walked up to the second floor where Min-jah's family doctor could be found.

Byung-woo lets out a frustrated grunt as his calls were being ignored. Clenching his fits he glares up at a gaggle of nervous employees waiting to be told what to do.

"Can anyone get a hold of his driver?" Byung-woo says through clenched teeth.

"Ah I did!" shouted an employee from the back.

"And?" Byung-woo says impatiently.

"Oh um w-well he said Chairman Lan g-gave him t-the day off..." the employee trailed off into a quiet whisper.

Byung-woo stood there looking at the employees with a blank stare. The employees awkwardly looked at each other and then back at the visibly angry Byung-woo.

I awkwardly stood off to the side of the room while Min-jah was sitting on the bed. The awkwardness grew as we just sat in the room and didn't talk, not sure how much more I could take. I felt like I had to say something. A knock followed by a doctor walking into the room broke the silence.

"Min Min," he smiled "What can I do for you today?" The doctor said as he sat down on a stool.

"First don't call me Min Min I'm not five anymore. Second, I think I have a cold." Min-jah said unamused to being treated like a child.

"How long have you felt like this?" asked the doctor.

"Um I'd say about two and a half weeks maybe?" Min-jah answered casually.

The doctor raises an eyebrow and silently tells Min-jah to remove his coat. The doctor then proceeds to do a general physical check up on him.

"What symptoms have you been having?" the doctor asks as he checks Min-jah's ears.

"It started off with just occasionally vomiting, some abdominal pain, oh and a strange rash that eventually went away on its own. But now my throat is killing me and I have this awful cough." Min-jah explains while the doctor checks the lymph nodes in his throat.

"Well I can't say for certain what it is without running some tests but I can tell you it's not a cold." The doctor said with concern in his voice. "Just hold tight and I'll have a nurse come in to draw some blood and get a urine sample from you."

Slightly concerned Min-jah agrees with the doctor. He sighs as the doctor leaves the room.

"I know, I know. I should have come way earlier." Min-jah says not even looking at me. "But I have over 7,000 people and their families who depend on me. I couldn't afford to get sick so I just ignored it." he continued to explain dropping his head.

The unexplained sudden anger I felt while listening melted away as I looked at his disappointed face. With a sigh I looked away from him since I was unable to say anything to console him. A few minutes later a nurse comes in and hands Min-jah a cup and takes three vials full of blood.

"Doctor Hun says if you have the time to hang around for the results shouldn't take very long." The nurse says as she walks out the door.

Min-jah looks over at me as if to silently ask if it's okay. I smiled and shrugged in response. We had been waiting for half an hour when Min-jah had decided to lie down and fall asleep. I looked at him and could tell how exhausted he was by the dark circles under his eyes. I silently hoped the results would take longer just so he could continue to sleep. A light knock came from the door and I lightly tapped Min-jah's shoulder to wake him.

"I was hoping it was something else." Doctor Hun began dejectedly as soon as he walked in.

"What do you mean doctor?" Min-jah asked sleepily as he sat up.

"You have acute arsenic poisoning." Doctor Hun answered bluntly.

"What?" we both said shocked.

The doctor hands Min-jah the test results. While looking at the paper Min-jah began to become increasingly flustered.

"Luckily we can still treat it and it doesn't look like the levels are high enough to do any real damage internally." Doctor Hun quickly adds seeing Min-jah's face. "We do have to start treatment immediately."

Min-jah looks up at me as if he couldn't comprehend anything the doctor was saying to him.

"I-I- I don't understand where I would have come into contact with arsenic?" Min-jah finally manages to say through the shock.

"It's hard to say exactly but unfortunately based on how long and the dosage you have been exposed to it I'd lay my best guess on it being unintentional." Doctor Hun says gravely. "I mean unless someone is actually trying to kill you." He jokes

Min-jah and I quickly glanced over at each other as the doctor laughed off his own poorly told joke. With a white prescription bag in hand we slowly trudged out of the hospital.

"Are you really going to be okay?" I said quietly with my head down.

Min-jah smiled "Of course I just need to take these twice a day." The pills rattled together as he shook the bag comically. "Just until I figure out how I am being exposed and then I can start getting better." he finished confidently.

Not feeling the same confidence I flashed a halfhearted smile as we made our way to the car.

"Besides, I promised to play hooky with you remember?" Min-jah smiles mischievously as he unlocks the car. "So let's play hooky."

I couldn't help but laugh a little as he skipped excitedly toward the car. Our first stop was a high end hand tailored suit shop that I didn't even qualify to even be on the same street as. I looked at him nervously as he held the door of the store open.

"I'm looking for a suit." Min-jah says to the first person he sees.

"Of course right this way Sir." She answers as she goes to lead Min-jah to a rack.

"Oh not for me," Min-jah protests "it's for him." He says pointing at me.

Stunned, I quickly spun around on my heels to look at him. The sales lady looked me up and down and then with visible confusion looked at Min-jah with disbelief. Min-jah finds a seat as he shoos us away and grabs a magazine. Despite my protests I ended up in the dressing room with a multitude of different suits.

The first suit I tried on was a bright banana yellow mess. I was hesitant to even open the door of the dressing room. I shook my head as I showed Min-jah who looked like he was struggling not to laugh. Annoyed, I quickly stepped back into the room and tried another. The next one was an old gangster pinstripe suit that was only missing the fedora to complete the look.

I looked like a fool but I walked out to show him anyway. Immediately Min-jah let out a chuckle as he saw me. His eyes darted right and in a flash he jumped up and placed a hat on my head. I looked in the mirror to see a matching fedora on my head and we both busted out laughing. I continued to try one suit after another until we finally found the perfect one.

I walked out of the dressing room pulling the jacket on over my shoulders. I looked in the large mirror and what I saw I couldn't believe was my reflection. Wearing a pair of black dress shoes so shiny I could see my reflection, a dark navy blue suit that made my blue eyes look even brighter. I shifted my bangs just slightly so they were out of my eyes as I tried to tie the tie. Min-jah suddenly spun me around and pulled the tie out from around my neck and reached up and unbuttoned the top two buttons of my shirt.

"Looks much better this way." he said with a grin as he straightened out the creases.

"So close" I thought as I looked into his eyes as he fixed my clothes when he suddenly looked back into mine making my heart skip a beat. My face suddenly felt hot and my heart started pounding like crazy. I stepped away with a soft cough and started breathing heavily to control my heartbeat. I placed my hand over my chest convinced I was about to have a heart attack with how fast it was beating.

"I'll take the whole suit. We'll wear it out." Min-jah says to the sales women handing over a black card.

He drove me to a luxurious restaurant that I had only read about in magazines. We stopped in front as a valet driver rushed up and opened my door. I got out nervously as Min-jah handed over the keys with a smile to another driver. I watched as Min-jah started walking when he suddenly stopped and turned to look at me and waved for me to hurry.

"Chairman Lan," a man bowed to greet us at the door, "I didn't know you were coming-"

"I'm not here on official business just here to eat." Min-jah interrupted "Just treat me like any other guest today Mr. Park."

"Ah ha of course Sir." he chuckled nervously as he showed us to a table.

There was light music playing that quietly complimented the light chatter from the other guests enjoying their meal. I looked around in awe to see a glittery world so fragile that it seemed as if one wrong move and it would shatter into a million pieces. I fidgeted uncomfortably in my seat as the waiter handed us a menu. I instantly gasped in disbelief at the prices for the food on the menu.

"Chairman Lan," I whispered harshly from behind my menu. "You can't be serious?!"

"Stop being so formal," he pouted, "order whatever you want. Might just be your only chance to eat from here."

I groaned anxiously as I looked back at the menu a little disgruntled at the fact he was right. I gulped as I read the word steak and glanced up from the menu to look at Min-jah. He looked at me with an encouraging smile as he waved down the waiter.

I leaned back and with a smile let out a satisfied sigh as a waiter cleared the dirty dishes. Min-jah thanked the waiter with a nod as he finished his drink.

"Would you like to order dessert?" Min-jah chuckles as he watches me rub my stomach.

"Oh no, I couldn't eat another bite." I laughed as I sat up straight.

Min-jah's phone began to ring again for the millionth time since this morning. Annoyed, he quickly sent the call to voicemail and paid the bill.

"What if it's important?" I asked quietly looking at his phone.

"If it was I'm sure Byung-woo would have already sent someone to come get me." he laughed as we walked out of the restaurant.

"You aren't going to get into trouble for playing hooky, are you?" I asked as the valet driver drove up with the car.

"Haha," he laughed out loud, "I am the CEO if anything I'll just have to listen to Byung-woo scold me half the night."

I chuckled at his unyielding carefree attitude as we got into the car. I stared out the car window absentmindedly as we drove down the road. Starting to feel sad as the day was coming to an end I accidentally let an audible sigh slip catching Min-jah's attention.

"Hey-" Min-jah started to say

"Do you still think I'm the one who's trying to kill you?" I asked bluntly, interrupting him.

"What?" Min-jah squeaked out in surprise.

"Back at the hotel you asked me if I was trying to kill you. Do you still think that?" I asked, staring at him intensely.

Trying to keep his eyes on the road and look at me, he didn't answer for quite some time.

"No." he finally says

I looked at his face as he watched the road to see if he was lying. Min-jah looked at me from the corner of his eye and smiled softly at me.

"Honest." he said.

I sat back in the seat still a little skeptical about his answer. I narrowed my eyes and looked at him sideways unconvinced.

"There is one thing I'm curious about though." Min-jah says as he switches lanes.

"What's that?" I said, still squinting at him.

"How did you know?" Min-jah asks looking directly at me.

"Ah..." I quickly looked away, "about that... it's kinda hard to explain..." I mumbled as I pulled up my hood to hide behind.

"What do you mean?" he asks.

"Well it's just not that easy to understand." I said anxiously.

"Try me." he quickly darted back.

I groaned as I slowly turned back to look at him.

"You will believe me?" I softly asked as I looked at him.

"You have no reason to lie to me so why wouldn't I?" Min-jah said with a smile.

I looked away from him nervously as a million questions began to flood into my head. Would he actually believe me? Will he think I'm crazy? Would he avoid me like everyone else? What if he gets scared of me? What if he doesn't want to see me again? I looked up at him and seeing his smile made all the worries slightly fade away. Will it really be okay? I bit my lip as I looked at him having made my decision.

"Okay but we should pull over somewhere." I said shakily.

Byung-woo sighed heavily as once again his call went straight to voicemail. He leaned back in his office chair looking out at the employees who can only do half of their job because Min-jah was not there. He grabs a stack of binders and walks down the hall to Min-jah's office. He placed the stack down next to two more large stacks on the desk and shakes his head disapprovingly as he walks out.

I turned towards him, opened my mouth and then quickly closed it as I shook my head and turned away from him. I rubbed my hands together slowly as we sat in silence on a bench. Still trying to work up the nerve to tell him about this curse I was born with I took a deep breath.

"What is it?" Min-jah asks impatiently, breaking the silence.

"It's..." I sighed, "it's kinda hard to believe..." I said discouragingly.

"I'll believe you no matter what." Min-jah states with a soft grin.

I chuckled as I let out a big breath. Still a little concerned I looked at him and gulped.

"Okay..." I start, "I knew because I saw it." I blurted bluntly.

"You saw it? As in you can see the future?" he asked flabbergasted.

"Um well no... not exactly..." I said flustered.

He looked at me very confused and I looked away trying to sort out in my head how I would explain it. I took my hand out of my pocket and rubbed my mouth. Then it hit me.

"Look," I held up my hand, "When I have any kind of physical contact with someone I can see how that person will die." I said a little too loudly as people were starting to stare.

"So that night when you brushed my bangs with your hand I saw you getting shot in the head." I continued softly. "The second shot was because I touched your ankle when you rolled over. However my visions don't actually tell me when or where they will happen, with you I guess we just got lucky? I can also feel all the pain and their emotions as the person goes through it so that's a little inconvenient."

Min-jah sat there trying to comprehend this seemingly unfathomable situation. A little concerned that he hadn't said a word as I rambled I waved my hand in front of his face. Knocked out of his trance he instinctively moved away. I retracted my hand and slowly placed it on my lap in response. Preparing myself for the worst I squeezed my hands together and closed my eyes.

"Have you always been able to do this?" he asked in a serious tone.

"What?... Ah y-yes." I stuttered out surprised.

"Ha that's pretty cool!" he shouted excitedly.

"Ha." I said with a sigh as I began to smile.

"Who all knows you can do this?" he asks as he scoots closer to me.

"Uh n-noone." I said nervously.

"What? Why?" he asked shockingly disappointed.

"Ah... well when I was a young child people suspected I was a little different. It wasn't until I was old enough to start school they found out how different." I looked down dejectedly, "There was this older kid who lived next door, he would always bring me treats and hold my hand while we walked home after school. One day the vision suddenly changed from peacefully dying in his sleep at an old age, to him being pushed off a cliff no older than 11 years old. That was when I learned that these visions could change. Terrified I pleaded with him, his parents and with mine to believe me. Being only a child, it fell on deaf ears chalked up to me just having a wild imagination. A week later, the day of his 11th birthday, on a school camping trip to the mountains the boy gets pushed off a cliff and falls to his death. Shortly after I began to be known as a 'devil child' and my parents were ostracized as devil worshippers. I think they put up with it for maybe six months?" I laughed bitterly. "Then they dropped me off at the closest orphanage and disappeared. I was adopted out a few times but they always ended with the family not being able to handle it and bringing me back. One family seemed like the perfect fit until I had a vision of the whole family being murdered one night. I told them and they became very scared and quickly took me back immediately. Only to be viciously murdered by a runaway convict a week later. After that crazy rumors started to spread and I was continuously bullied, beaten, and even locked in small dark places by other kids and sometimes even by adults. I was never adopted out again." I said broken-heartedly.

I sniffled and wiped my eyes laughing at myself for still getting emotional about all of it. Feeling very vulnerable I habitually flipped up my hood to hide my face.

"Weren't you scared I would react the same way?" Min-jah asked softly.

"Petrified." I said shakily. "But, something feels different with you."

"Different?" he asks.

"I want you to know. I strangely don't want to have to hide anything. I feel uneasy if I have to lie to you. So I don't want to have to." I said shyly.

"Then tell me everything." he says ever so sweetly with a smile.

And then as if I was a simple piece of butter in a heated pan. I instantly began to melt with that smile.

"O-okay." I answered in a low whisper.

We sat on that park bench which felt like forever looking up at the stars in the sky as I told him everything. All the torment and suffering I had endured over the years. How terrified I am being alone and how terrified I am being with people. Afterwards I told him how I use this curse to help people silently instead. When the sudden thought that I might be able to help Min-jah figure out how he was being poisoned popped into my head.

"I might be able to help you." I said hopeful.

"Help me? With what?" Min-jah asked with a chuckle.

"Help you figure out how you are being poisoned." I said a little too cheerfully.

Min-jah laughed as I realized how excited I sounded I shyly turned away from him.

"Just. Here." I said frustrated as I grabbed his hand.

I let his hand go and started coughing violently confused. I looked up at him.

"What did you see?" he asked.

"I just saw you eating and drinking different things, never the same thing twice. The only thing that doesn't change is where you are." I explained, still coughing.

"Where am I?" he urges.

"In a large room always sitting at a wooden desk." I said confused.

Min-jah lets out a sigh as he stands up and tugs his jacket tighter around him. I looked at him worried that he doesn't actually believe me.

"It's getting late, do you want me to take you home?" he asked as he stood there.

"Oh no could I get you to drop me off at the bakery?" I said with my chest still tight.

"This late?" he asked questioningly.

"I have to walk Yuki-ji home, she closed tonight." I said kicking a small pebble.

"Why do you have to walk her home?" he questioned.

"So I should just let a young woman walk home alone in the dark?" I joked.

Flustered Min-jah looks away from me unable to answer.

"Ha ha," I laughed, "I had a vision that someone attacked her one night on her way home." I explained.

"What?!" he exclaims.

"Relax, I roughly know when. I just figured I might be able to deter him if I stick annoyingly close to her by walking her home every night." I answered confidently.

Frowning, I could tell he didn't like the idea but couldn't flat out reject it either. I smiled as I looked at him seriously trying to think of another plan.

"I've done this over a dozen times." I tried to reassure him.

"Doesn't mean it's not dangerous." he scolded as we got into the car.

"I know." I agreed, "But I'm always careful when it comes to these kinds of things."

Not convinced he put the car in drive and we left. When we arrived he hesitantly put the car in park. I grabbed the shopping bag that held my new clothes from the back. Seeing Min-jah's expression of concern, I placed my hand on his arm and lightly squeezed as I opened the car door. He quickly pulls me back inside the car.

"Seriously just let me drive you." he protests.

"I'll be fine." I argue as I slip out of his grip. "So you actually believe me?"

"It's a little hard to swallow but it's the only thing that actually makes a little sense." he answers looking at me.

I smile as the tightness in my chest loosens. He looks at me beggingly as I step out of the car.

"I still have to go." I chuckle as I close the door.

With an exaggerated sigh he throws himself against his seat. I chuckled as I waved goodbye and he drove away.

"Who's that?" comes a voice from behind me.

"Gahh!" I shout.

"Sorry, haha." Yuki-ji laughs.

"He's a friend." I answered with a smile. "You ready?"

Knowing he wasn't going to be able to sleep Min-jah drives to the office instead of going home. With a light knock on the glass door he smiles apologetically as the old security guard walks over to unlock the door. He walks into his office and flips on the light to see four large stacks of paperwork that needed to be gone through. He takes off his jacket and loosens his tie as he begins to work. Half way through the second stack his phone rings with a message.

> **I'm home. Thank you for today. Goodnight.**

With a giddy smile Min-jah replies quickly and goes back to working. Laying in bed hugging Mr. Snuggles I smiled as my phone buzzed.

Anytime. Goodnight. ☺

CHAPTER 6

Byung-woo is greeted by a crowd of employees standing in front of the elevator trying to catch a glimpse of something. He lets out an exasperated sigh as he pushes through the crowd to see what they were all looking at. Shocked, he stood in awe like the other onlookers as Min-jah stood up with paperwork in his hand. A dozen or more stacks of paper on the meeting room table he was sorting out a bunch of paperwork. His hair was tousled, his sleeves rolled up, and the top few buttons undone on his shirt.

"How long has he been here?" Byung-woo finally asks after staring.

"No idea, I got here at 6AM and he was already like this." said one female onlooker as she swooned.

Byung-woo flashed a look of shock and disgust at her as he squeezed his way in front of the crowd. Annoyed he chuckled as he looked at his watch seeing that no one was working and it was already 7:30AM.

"Okay." Byung-woo claps loudly, "Let's get to work, yeah?" he asked sarcastically as he shoos them away.

He flashes a quick glare at Min-jah as the crowd reluctantly disperses. He walks into the meeting room and quickly draws the blinds so the stragglers have no choice but to get to work. He immediately focuses all his attention on Min-jah before the door could click closed.

"And just where did you disappear to yesterday?" Byung-woo hisses.

"AH! Byung-woo you are finally here!" he smiles, not breaking his pace.

"Right. Don't try to change the subject. Answer my-" Byung-woo breaks off as Min-jah isn't listening.

Min-jah grabs more papers and continues to sign and sort them, not paying any attention to Byung-woo.

"How long have you been here?" Byung-woo asked, perplexed.

"Um since eleven?" he answered, not stopping.

"A-all night?" Byung-woo stuttered out in shock.

"Yeah." he stops to drink coffee only to find his cup is empty.

Min-jah hands his empty cup to Byung-woo nodding quickly for a refill. Baffled by the situation, Byung-woo grabs the cup out of Min-jah's shaky hand. He cocks his head quickly as he turns around to walk out to refill Min-jah's cup.

"Oh!" Min-jah shouts, "I need you to be the soul person who handles all my food and drinks from now on." he hastily spits out.

"Um why?" Byung-woo asked with slight annoyance as he stopped the door from closing on him.

"I think someone is poisoning my food." he says flat out.

Byung-woo flinches slightly before he starts to nervously chuckle walking back into the room.

"What makes you think that?" he asks unconvinced.

"Went to the doctor yesterday..." Min-jah says distractedly, "He told me I have acute arsenic poisoning."

"And what makes you think it's in your food?" he asks nervously.

"Well how else would I come into contact with it?" Min-jah says firmly as he finally stops working.

"What about me? I always eat lunch with you!" Byung-woo shrieks.

"I'm sure you are fine, besides you haven't been sick like me." Min-jah states matter of factly.

"Haha guess that's true. Just making enemies everywhere you go, don't you?" Byung-woo chuckles as he walks out.

Byung-woo places Min-jah's coffee mug down on the counter a little too hard as he sighs.

"Seon." he calls hastily.

"Yes sir?" A petite young woman with long black hair answers almost immediately.

"From now on I'll handle all food and drink orders for Chairman Lan." he says exhaustedly.

"Ah did I mess it up?" she panics.

"Nothing like that," he chuckles "just some unnecessary pickiness is all." he says through a forced smile.

Byung-woo returns to the office with lunch for Min-jah when he finds Min-jah sleeping peacefully on the couch in the office. He quietly places the food on the desk so as to not wake him. Byung-woo tip toes over to the couch and gazes at Min-jah as he sleeps. Min-jah suddenly shifts making his hair fall slightly over his face. Softly Byung-woo shifts the hair back, with a soft smile, to its original position before lightly stroking Min-jah's cheek waking him up.

"Come and eat then go home and sleep for a few hours." Byung-woo says softly. "You have done all the important work for today."

Min-jah smiles a goofy smile as he stretches out on the couch. Even though he hadn't been asleep for long he sat up to reveal his messy bed hair. Byung-woo chuckled lightly at the sleepy Min-jah as he walked over with the food. Having woken up slightly after eating he said goodbye to his employees and left. Min-jah makes a quick dash to his bed where he collapsed on top of it without washing up or changing.

I sighed as my messages to him were left unread, disappointed I put my phone back into my locker as my lunch break was coming to an end. I tied my apron around me as I walked back into the busy kitchen.

"I'm back." I hollered over the noise.

"Perfect!" Fei says ecstatically as he pushes a couple dozen cupcakes into my station from his.

I flash a playful glare at him while putting on gloves. He flashes a wide toothy smile in response. I rolled my eyes and chuckled as I grabbed a bag of frosting and started piping a white flower on the first cupcake. Hanging my apron in my locker disheartedly, I let out a sigh as I still haven't heard from Min-jah all day. I gathered my things and started to head out of the locker room when I bumped into Yuki-ji.

"Oh Joon! You don't have to take me home tonight going to spend the night with friends and go to the concert together tomorrow." she squeals excitedly as she runs down the hall.

She stops mid run turns around with a giant smile and squeals loudly one last time before she takes off again. I laughed lightly as I watched her run away down the small corridor. I pushed open the alleyway door when a gust of wind almost knocked me off my feet. A crackly voice then echoed inside my head so clearly I was sure someone was in the alley with me.

"Make sure you bring your bonded selection with you." the crackly voice echoed quickly and then the wind stopped.

I stood there silently in the dark alley reminded of the strange dream I had of the shabby looking store. Unsure what the voice meant about the 'bonded selection' I made my way to the bus stop. I stepped onto the crowded bus swiping my wallet as I made my way through the sea of people. Unable to find an open seat I was left standing. The words bonded selection echoed in my thoughts as I looked around the bus seeing couples, mothers with their children, and even an old blind man with his four legged companion. I pulled out my phone and made a call.

Min-jah flinches awake as his phone starts to loudly ring from his jacket pocket. He pats around on the bed trying to find the source only to realize it was coming from across the room. He groans loudly as he drags himself out of bed reluctantly and stumbles toward the noise. The ringing stops just as he reaches out to grab his jacket. Defeated he drops his head with a sigh as he turns around to go back to bed when it starts ringing again.

"Hello." Min-jah says with a sleepy voice.

"Min-jah?" comes the familiar voice through the phone.

Min-jah's eyes shoot wide open as he quickly pulls the phone away from his ear to check who is calling.

"H-hello? Are you there?" I ask.

"Y-yes I'm here." he quickly answers.

"I think I need to take you somewhere." I say cryptically.

"You think?" Min-jah questions.

"Yeah, can you meet me at my place in about an hour?" I ask as I try to keep myself from falling.

"Uh yeah, okay, sure." Min-jah agrees right away.

"Great see you then." I say happily as I hang up the phone.

Min-jah stands in the middle of the room processing the conversation before he quickly darts into the bathroom. Only having enough time to dry his hair Min-jah fixes his bangs in the rearview mirror. I knocked on the car window using my knuckle and waved a pair of flashlights in the air as Min-jah looked up at me.

"We can walk." I say as I open his door.

I handed over a flashlight as he reluctantly got out of the car. I urged him to follow me as I clicked on my flashlight and started walking down the dark street.

"Are you sure we are going the right way?" Min-jah asked as he looked at the surrounding buildings that were looking more and more abandoned the farther we went. Shining the light on the closest street sign and quickly looking back to my phone.

"Yes, it says it's just right up here on the next street." I say hoping I didn't get us lost.

As we got closer to the end of the street, we noticed a familiar warm glow from lights around the corner. With hopeful smiles we hurried towards the sudden glow. Turning the corner I stopped as I noticed the sign hanging above the door that read MAMA TOOKIE. We slowly made our way to the front of the shabby looking building.

"What is this place?" Min-jah asks softly.

"I don't actually know I had a strange dream about this place once. And then something weird happened when I was leaving work today." I explained as we both stood there.

"Wait... a dream?" Min-jah says, recalling his own dream.

"Yeah..." I say trailing off.

The door suddenly begins to creak open as a black cat with solid bright green eyes appears staring at us. The cat meows softly and turns away heading back inside the door almost as if it was inviting us in. Min-jah slowly pushes the door open wide enough for us to squeeze inside. Inside were several shelves that were filled with various obviously homemade items. Some shelves were overstuffed with handmade clay pots while others have accumulated a thick layer of dust as if they had been completely forgotten. Along the ends of each shelf were old wooden barrels filled with clear crystals of various shapes and sizes.

As we made our way through the aisles looking at all the strange yet slightly appealing clay pieces the cat meowed again. Quickly looking over, the cat was sitting on a counter that was nestled in the way back of the store. He closed his eyes and began to purr loudly as the curtain covering the hallway behind him suddenly shifted. Thinking it was just a trick of the light we slowly made our way towards the counter. The curtain moves again as the cat flicks his tail and turns to look.

"Mizuki, why did you turn on the lights?" comes a crackly voice as the curtain is flung wide open.

Mizuki meows once in response to a small old woman appearing out of the darkness. She had long grey hair that was loosely tied back with a black ribbon. She stood with a wooden cane as she walked out of the hallway. Wearing a necklace with a gold chain that had a pure black crystal hanging from it and a light pink nightgown with matching slippers with her head down she continued to talk to the cat.

"What do you mean we have guests?" she says as she lifts her head revealing her bright light blue eyes.

Mizuki begins to purr as she stares at me and Min-jah as we awkwardly stare back at her.

"The bestowed." She whispers out softly.

Finding ourselves suddenly sitting at a dining room table as she made us some tea. Mizuki climbs onto my lap and purrs as I start to pet him. I look around the small but cute room that was decorated with dozens of small cat figurines and photos of her life on every surface.

"I'll have to apologize on behalf of Mizuki." she says sweetly from the kitchen.

"Apologize?" I questioned as I continued to pet him.

"Yes, he must have led you two here early. You see I wasn't expecting to meet you boys for another four years at least." she explains as she walks over with the tea. "But Mizuki has always been very impatient."

"I don't understand." I said as I looked at the cat purring in my lap.

"Joon let me explain." she says as she sits down.

I quickly looked over at Min-jah perplexed and a little startled as she said my name.

"How do you know his name?" Min-jah interrupts coldly.

"Where are my manners!" she laughs "The overly friendly one there is Mizuki and my name is Mama Tookie."

"That doesn't answer my question." Min-jah growls as he quickly grabs my arm and stands up.

Pulling me behind him Min-jah slowly begins to back away from Mama Tookie. Mizuki suddenly begins to growl and hiss as Min-jah grabs a lamp from the side table.

"Now, now let's just calm down so I can explain." Mama Tookie urges as she tries to defuse the tension.

Mizuki begins to lower his growl as Mama Tookie picks him up and pets him. Min-jah slowly places the lamp back down as she walks back to the table. Still not convinced Min-jah doesn't let me come out from behind him as we walk back.

"This is good, very good." Mama Tookie says with a smile as she puts Mizuki down.

"What are you talking about?" Min-jah asks annoyed.

"Please have a seat and I'll explain I promise." she urges.

Reluctantly Min-jah lets me sit back down. Mama Tookie giggles a childish giggle as she looks at Min-jah who slowly sits back down.

"I was born as a bestowed too." she begins.

Min-jah and I stared at her, unblinking unsure of how to respond.

"I must say it was a little concerning the selected bonded was a human and of the same sex to boot. But based off its quick reaction to protect the bestowed I'm sure this will be a very strong bond." she said with a sigh of relief.

"Wait a minute." I finally said confused "What do you mean a bestowed?"

"Someone bestowed with the gift to see death from a single touch." she confirmed.

"W-what are you-" I said nervously as I leaned closer to Min-jah.

"There's no point in trying to hide it dear, I know." she says with a sigh.

"H-how?" I asked softly.

"The beautiful genetic deformity that we share is the mark." she says pointing to her eyes.

"There a-are others?" I asked, shocked.

"Not exactly, only two bestowed exist at the same point in time. One always much younger than the other." she says as she gestures to me and then herself. "We don't just appear willy-nilly."

"How come I'm only meeting you right now? You clearly knew I existed and close by." I snapped.

"There are certain rules that a guider, such as myself, and a bonded have to abide by." she says understandingly. "As a guider I must only carefully watch and guide the bestowed, must never interfere." she continued cryptically.

"Watch? So you have always known who I was?" I questioned.

"Yes. I have been silently following the bestowed since its birth." she said quietly.

Completely overwhelmed I sunk into my chair unable to ask any more questions. Glancing over at me Min-jah squeezed my arm to comfort me and took over.

"Earlier you said we were early, what did you mean by that?" Min-jah asks.

"Like I said Mizuki must have led the bestowed here, at the age of 27 is when the bestowed is supposed to be strong enough to form the link with the selected bonded and decide how to use the gift. I am to guide the bestowed on how to form the link and start the beginning of its life." Mama Tookie explains as Mizuki jumps up on the table.

"I have already decided how I want to use this curse." I interjected quickly.

"Y-you have?" Mama Tookie asks, surprised.

"What do you mean by selected bonded?" Min-jah continues to pry.

"The selected bonded is the living thing the bestowed has decided it never wants to be apart from. For me it is Mizuki." she continues explaining.

"So he's going to have to come back with his selected bonded or whatever in four years?" Min-jah asks confused.

"Well, not exactly since the bestowed already brought the selected bonded." she smiles "Although quite a young bestowed, I strangely feel this bestowed might be strong enough already." she says enthusiastically.

"Wait, you're saying I'm the selected bonded?" Min-jah squeaks out.

"Honestly, Bestowed are you sure this is the one?" Mama Tookie asks apprehensively glancing at me.

Unsure of how to respond, I glance at Min-jah and then back to Mama Tookie. She shakes her head as she stands up and starts walking past us.

"Follow me." she says quickly.

Disappearing through the curtain leading into the hallway back to the store we both stand up and slowly follow behind her.

"So you don't want to be apart from me?" he whispered mockingly into my ear.

"I-I…" I said flustered covering my ear. "You are the first person who didn't run or come at me with a crucifix." I managed to whisper out as we walked

I quickly elbowed him in his side as I could feel my face turning red from him standing too close. Following closely behind her we walked back into the store where she grabbed a handful of clear crystals and waved me over. I hesitantly walked over to her where she grabbed my hand and removed my glove. I quickly pulled my hand away, she reacted faster than I expected by smacking my forehead and pulling my hand back.

Min-jah quickly covers his mouth with his hand to hide the chuckle he accidently let slip. I glared over at him, confused and rubbing my forehead. Mama Tookie then began placing crystals in my hand one at a time before she found what she was looking for. She hands a matching crystal to Min-jah with a smile as she pushes us out from behind the counter. Confused, we stood there holding the crystals in our hands staring at her.

"Mizuki!" she shouts loudly "be a dear and go get me the bonding thread." she commands softly. With a disgruntled meow Mizuki disappears down the hallway.

"What you have in your hands is called a bonding crystal. The pair of identical crystals will give you the progress of your bond. Well as long as you are both alive and wearing them that is." Mizuki jumps on the counter with two matching gold necklaces. "For example," she moves Mizuki's fur to show an identical black crystal attached to a gold necklace wrapped around his collar like the one she was wearing. "If I take mine off…" she removes her necklace and the color from both crystals instantly fades away. "The crystals start off with different colors." she explained as she put hers back on. "The bonded's crystal will be a shade of blue and the bestowed's is a color that stems from the individuals gift."

The crystal around her neck turned red and then to a deep purple before going back to the solid black. I looked at the crystal in my hand and noticed that it was no longer clear but was a dark yellow color. I quickly glanced over at Min-jah's crystal but it was still clear. Mama Tookie smiled softly as she watched me.

"When the bond gets stronger the colors will begin to mix. The stronger the bond the darker the color. The darker the color-"

"The harder to break the bond." Min-jah interrupts as he stares at the crystal.

"Here," she reached out her hand for the crystals "Now let's have the bestowed officially select the bonded." she said with a smile as she places the crystals in the necklaces and hands them back to me. "All that has to be done now is to place the crystal on the bonded."

I turned toward Min-jah and nervously walked closer to him. I looked up at him and started to blush as he was staring straight at me. I raised the necklace up and nervously started to place the crystal around his neck. Scared he might be able to hear how loud my heart was beating, I quickly placed the necklace and stepped away. The crystal instantly began to fill with a rich blue hue as soon as I let it go.

"Now as long as the link to the bonded grows the bestowed can begin to control the gift." Mama Tookie says happily.

"Control it?" I asked, surprised.

"Yes, the stronger the bond the bestowed has with the bonded the easier the gift will be to control. In order to obtain a strong bond there will be some work to do." Mama Tookie explains. "Right now the bond is easily breakable but it has the potential to be stronger than even mine and Mizuki's." she chuckles.

"How?" I asked.

"There are three different types of bonds that can be formed. The weakest being a mental bond meaning to have the ability to know, just by looking, what is on one another's minds. A stronger one would be an emotional bond, being able to express and understand one another's feelings. The strongest bond would be a physical one, being able to comfortably touch one another often." Mama Tookie explains "To have an incredibly strong bond one must have bonded on all three levels. Unlike me and Mizuki who only have the mental and physical bond."

Mizuki meows as he hops on the counter and nuzzles against Mama Tookie.

"What's the fastest way to have a strong bond?" I said excitedly.

"A bond doesn't have a quick track. They need to be formed naturally over time, it can't be forced." Mama Tookie warns. "If the bond is forced the bond will break."

"Right." I said disappointedly.

"Don't worry bestowed, surprisingly this generation is stronger than I had anticipated. Will get there much sooner than I did." Mama Tookie says with a smile as she points toward my necklace.

I glanced down at the crystal to see a deep green color coming up from the bottom of the crystal already. I looked over at Min-jah who was smiling while looking at his crystal. We said our goodbyes to Mizuki and Mama Tookie and walked out of the store and into the night. While walking I noticed Min-jah wasn't with me. I turned around to see him and Mama Tookie still talking in front of the store.

"The role as a bonded is more important than just allowing the bestowed to have a chance at a regular life." Mama Tookie says in a grave tone.

"What do you mean?" Min-jah asks concerned

"As I stated earlier about the rules that need to be abided, the bonded needs to protect the bestowed as if its life depends on it." Mama Tookie squeezes his arm, "in the case a bestowed might die because the bonded failed to protect, the crystal will as a last resort."

"The crystal?" Min-jah repeated softly.

"The crystal is a frightfully powerful force that will do anything to protect the bestowed once activated. As a last resort the crystal will take the life of the bonded in order to save the bestowed. As a punishment for not following through with its duties." Mama Tookie says in an icy tone. "The bonded must protect the bestowed at all costs or it will cost the ultimate price."

Min-jah stares at Mama Tookie as she places a small bag in his hand.

"Take this if the bonded wishes to understand more." she closes his hand and squeezes.

Min-jah glances over at me with a pained expression as he says his last goodbyes and walks away. I cocked my head sideways in confusion as he gradually walked closer to me.

"What was that?" I asked as he got closer.

"It's nothing." he quickly replied as he continued walking.

I glanced back to see Mama Tookie was gone and all the lights had already been shut off. I picked up my pace to catch up to Min-jah who had continued walking down the dark street.

CHAPTER 7

Standing outside my door I waved goodbye to Min-jah one last time as he drove away. I smiled, staring at my hand as I walked inside trying to imagine what it would be like to not have to stress over accidentally touching someone. Be able to receive a high five or simply shake hands with another person. To be able to hold someone's hand without seeing how they would die. In an instant Min-jah's face popped into my head making my cheeks flush. I shook the image out of my head embarrassingly as I walked into the restroom.

I flopped down on my bed slowly drying my hair as my mind raced with thoughts of all the little things I've never done. I rolled over to grab Mr. Snuggles when the crystal necklace hit my hand. I gazed at it and rolled the crystal between my fingertips. Wondering how I could make our bond stronger, I drifted off to sleep.

Min-jah tosses his car keys on the small shelf right next to his door as he kicks off his shoes. Slipping into his house shoes he sits down on the white couch in his living room as Mama Tookie's last words to him echoed in his head. He pulls out the small Ziplock bag that contained a small clear blue pill out of his pocket. Sitting there he pushed the pill around the small bag while staring at it intensely.

Sitting on his bed drying his hair Min-jah stares at the pill sitting on his night stand. He frustratedly grabbed the pill and hesitated for a second before he tossed it into his mouth. Swallowing he sits and waits for something to happen. Making a clicking noise with his tongue irritated Min-jah stands up in a rush suddenly feeling dizzy and falls back onto the bed. The room starts to spin as his body begins to feel heavy he slowly passes out as the pill takes its effect.

Min-jah finds himself in a poorly lit nursery room of a hospital. Looking around he sees two babies swaddled and sleeping next to each other in the same bed. Taking a closer look he realizes the name tags on the bed, one with his name while the other had Joon's.

"From the moment of birth the bonded was already predetermined." Mama Tookie's voice echoed

Min-jah swiftly swirls around to find Mama Tookie standing in the doorway of the nursery.

"The bonded has already been saved by the bestowed more than once, right?" Mama Tookie questions.

"No just once." Min-jah corrects her.

Mama Tookie smiles at him coyly as she opens a door to the outside. A bright light flooded into the room causing Min-jah to cover his eyes. He opens them and he's standing in a crowded street in the middle of winter. He couldn't believe his eyes as a thirteen year old Min-jah came walking towards him.

The young Min-jah walks past him angrily rubbing his hands together because he forgot to wear gloves. When he is suddenly knocked to the ground as he's about to viciously vent out his anger, young Min-jah looks up and sees a boy. Standing in front of him was a scrawny boy about the same age wearing a thin black jacket with the ends frayed and covered in dirt, his pants had multiple holes in them, his shoes looked like they were barely hanging together, and in his hand was a brand new brown teddy bear that was wearing a sweater with a heart on it. The boy offered out his hand while apologizing for knocking him down. The boy's hand looked as white as the snow on the ground reaching up and unhesitantly he takes his hand and pulled himself off the ground.

When young Min-jah let the boy's hand go he was shocked at how cold it was. He looked up to see the boy was already gone. Unable to find him, the young Min-jah shrugs and continues walking. After several minutes out of nowhere the scrawny boy suddenly grabs the hood of his jacket and yanks him backward. As they both fall into the snow a neon store sign comes crashing down a few feet in front of the young Min-jah. Almost as if they mastered the art of camouflage four large men suddenly appeared and gathered around the young Min-jah. Startled he quickly looks for the scrawny boy but only catches a glimpse of him as he fwips up the hood to his jacket covering his face and disappears into the crowd.

"More than once." Mama Tookie says mockingly.

"You're telling me that the nearly frozen scrawny boy from ten years ago was Joon?" he asks shocked.

"Mhmm." Mama Tookie shrugs as she walks away from the scene.

Suddenly back inside Min-jah's room Mama Tookie sits on the bed next to Min-jah's unconscious body.

"Just as the bonded is naturally drawn to the bestowed so is another. With all energy there are positive and negative forces." Mama Tookie says cryptically.

Listening to her every word Min-jah stands there and waits for her to explain.

"Bonded are what's known as the fated bond, the one who will love and protect the bestowed. While another will only hurt and destroy known as the ill-fated bond. Usually once the bonded destroys the ill-fated bond the bestowed is said to be safe for the rest of its life... but..." Mama Tookie trails off.

"But?" he renunciates.

"Something is different with this bestowed. Everything is done much sooner than predicted. Like the bond this bestowed has already decided years ago how to use the gift. This bestowed is much stronger than any predecessor." she says concerned.

"What does that mean for him?" Min-jah questions.

"For the bestowed I'm not sure. It's the bonded that I am worried about." Mama Tookie says looking at him.

"Me? Why me?" he wonders.

"With the way the bestowed chose to use the gift there will be many ill-fated bonds. I'm afraid it will be very tough for the bonded in the future." Mama Tookie explains.

"Well can't I just ask him to use it another way?" Min-jah questions.

"One must only guide-"

"-Not interfere. Yeah, yeah I got it." Min-jah interrupts. "Well I guess I better get my money's worth of all those kickboxing classes I have been taking." he says with a chuckle

Still a little concerned Mama Tookie nods her head and slowly disappears with a smile.

Mama Tookie wakes up laying in bed with a smile she reaches down and pets Mizuki purring he rolls over on his back guiding her hand to his stomach.

"The bonded appears to be stronger than I had originally expected as well." Mama Tookie says with a chuckle.

Startled by my alarm the next morning I woke up with the crystal in my hand. I stretched as I pulled myself out of bed to get ready for work. Min-jah, already on his way to the office, pulls out his phone with a grin as his thumbs move across the screen rapidly. The brakes squeal loudly as the bus came to a stop sounding like they hadn't been changed since public transportation became popular. I braced against the seat in front of me to prevent myself from sliding out of my seat as the bus slowly came to a complete stop. A buzzing sensation suddenly came from my jacket pocket. I smiled as I quickly retrieved the phone already knowing who it was.

Good morning. ☺

Good morning.

I've been thinking all night on how to make the bond
Stronger. What better way than with constant contact?

I can't have my phone when
I'm in the kitchen.

Okay... almost constant contact then. ☹

I shook my head with a smile sliding my phone back into my pocket and got off the bus. Walking down the alley to the employee entrance my phone vibrated again. My smile instantly fades away as I didn't recognize the number that was on the screen.

Hello there handsome... 😺
I finally found you.

I quickly turned around and checked the alley for other people seeing a figure as it slipped behind the corner of the alley. I darted toward the end of the alley to see a dozen or more people casually walking on the sidewalk. As I frantically look up and down the street my phone dings again.

Now Now, no need to rush we will see each other soon...

Afraid of being late again I pulled my jacket tighter around me as I turned to make my way down the alley again. I opened the door to find an overly excited Yuki-ji showing off her new hoodie she received from the concert. My problems instantly disappeared when I saw her wearing the pink hoodie. I was reminded that I still needed to stop her neighbor from trying to kill her and soon.

The day seemed to be over in the blink of an eye as I was already back at my locker gathering my things to go home. I reminded myself that I had a job to do slamming my locker closed with determination that I had to protect Yuki-ji. Zoned out like usual as Yuki-ji rambles on about how much fun she had. I said the occasional 'uh huh' and 'that's cool' to make it seem like I was actually listening as we carried on down the dark street towards her house.

"...you wouldn't believe how dreamy he actually is like up close. His pictures don't do him any justice, he is so much better in person..." Yuki-ji squeals.

I heard a sudden rustling coming from the tree line up the hill on our right. I slowed down as I looked in the direction of the noise.

"...he gave off a really creepy vibe at first but after I talked to him more I realized he was actually a really nice guy. He actually lives in this area too." Yuki-ji rambles.

"Huh?" I said quickly, pulling my attention to what she said.

"A volunteer at the animal shelter where I help out on my days off. He started coming a few weeks ago." she explained.

I shook my head as I had no idea how the conversation she was having with herself about the singer led to talking about another person. We reached the one streetlight that worked and her neighbor was nowhere to be seen.

"Where's your neighbor?" I asked as we passed under the light.

"His firm just picked up a major project starting today so he's going to be coming home late for the next couple of days." she said sadly. "Aw-wa I miss him already.. You know he thinks you have a crush on me." she blurts out jokingly.

"What?" I laughed "Why?"

"Because you go out of your way to bring me home every night." she giggles.

"Well I promise you that's not it." I said bluntly, shaking my head.

"Well good because I don't like you." she says sticking out her tongue playfully.

I wave goodbye as she goes inside glancing left and right before I turn around. Yuki-ji watches from the side of her living room window as he walks away. With a deep sigh, she walked away from the window and flopped down on the couch.

"So it's not because he likes me..." she mumbled sadly as she covers her face to stop the tears from falling.

I walked off the bus letting out an exhausted sigh as I rubbed the back of my neck. I opened my eyes to see Min-jah smiling at me from the bus stop bench.

"Surprise." he says sweetly with a smile.

Happier than I thought I would be to see him I smiled as I shyly looked down at my feet. We walked side by side slowly stealing little glances not saying anything.

"What are you doing here?" I finally asked.

"Well obviously I'm walking you home." he answered jokingly.

"Ha you know what I mean." I laughed.

"Well I uh... I guess I just missed you." he said quietly.

Although it was dark, I knew he was blushing and I desperately wished to see it.

"I missed you too..." I replied shyly with a smile.

Min-jah reached over and grabbed my hand tightly as we continued walking. Taken back by my heart skipping a beat and the sweet smile he was giving me I squeezed his hand back. I saw my apartment building up in the distance and felt a twinge of sadness as I would have to say goodbye already. Min-jah squeezed my hand and smiled as we continued to walk closer to the building. I smiled at him as I let go of his hand and started to walk away. I let out a gasp as I was suddenly swirled around by him grabbing my hand and pulling me, making me fall into his arms. I looked up at him surprised as he slowly lifted his hand up toward my face.

"It's okay with gloves right?" he asked softly.

Staring into his eyes I slowly nodded my head as he continued to move his hand closer. The leather from his glove felt rough against my skin as he lightly brushed my hair out of my face and stroked my cheek. I stared into his eyes as they quickly flickered as if he was trying to carve every detail of my face into his memory as we stood there. I could feel my face flush, my heart felt like it was about to beat right out of my chest but I couldn't find it in me to push myself away. His eyes looked like a pool of dark chocolate that I wanted to jump into and never come out.

I gulped as his lips that shined because of his Chapstick parted ever so slightly. When Min-jah's phone began to ring suddenly and loudly pulling me back to reality. He instantly releases me as he quickly answers the phone. Suddenly embarrassed I turned away from him wanting to disappear. Min-jah hangs up the phone with a sigh.

"Do you have to go?" I asked sadly.

"Yeah." he answered.

I couldn't help but frown even though I already knew the answer.

"Joon." Min-jah called as he grabbed my hand.

"Mmhm." I chuckled softly.

"Good night." he uttered sweetly as he kissed the top of my glove.

"Good night." I replied as my cheeks instantly became flushed.

Sitting on my bed towel drying my hair I replayed Min-jah kissing my hand in my head. I flopped on the bed with my hair still wet with a large grin and kicked my feet in the air. With a happy squeal I violently rolled around and kicked my feet until I wore myself out. I hugged Mr. Snuggles tightly as I giggled happily. My giddy smile began to fade as a daunting question found its way into my thoughts. Am I even allowed to be this happy?

Groaning softly and toss and turn as I started to have another nightmare. Surrounded by darkness I walked not knowing where I was headed. While walking something suddenly grabs me and pulls me down deeper into the darkness as if I was falling into a never ending hole.

"Found you..." a voice hisses in my ear.

My entire body felt heavy as I laid on the ground unable to move. My surroundings came in slow flashes of darkness as I laid there. I was outside as I saw a tree line, a broken street light, and the night sky swallowed in darkness everything disappeared. Slowly the darkness receded, I saw my hand struggling to reach a small flashing square of light as the darkness crept back. The sound of my breathing echoed in my ears louder and louder with every wave of darkness.

The darkness lifted again and I saw the same small square of light but closer, it was my phone, Min-jah's name flashed across the screen at 11:00PM. I tried desperately to get my hand to move before the darkness could swallow me again. My finger was right above the green answer button when the darkness instantly rushed over me. My breathing still echoing in my ears became quieter until there was nothing, no noise, just empty darkness.

I woke up with a deep gasp laying on my back covered in a cold sweat. I rolled over grabbing Mr. Snuggles and pulling him close. As I close my eyes to go back to sleep I notice my phone flashing on my bedside table. I reach over and quickly unlock it to see two unread messages. I opened the message to see a picture of me and Yuki-ji smiling at work that had been taken from a short distance away followed by a text message.

Why are you always with her?

Unfazed by the apparent neighbor's attempt to scare me I locked my phone tossing it back on the table and rolled over in bed.

Standing in front of the mirror I looked at my roughly tousled hair serves me right for going to bed with wet hair. The faucet on the sink squeaked as I reached over to turn it on. Reaching for a towel blindly I managed to quickly fix my bed head. While drying my hair I looked down and noticed my crystal was half dark green now. I smiled softly as I continued to dry my hair.

While finishing getting dressed my phone dings with a smile I quickly picked it up. Realizing it was from the same unknown number from before I hesitantly opened the message. Upon opening it I see a picture of Min-jah surprising me at the bus stop last night. My phone dings repeatedly as more pictures of us from last night flooded my screen. The last picture I received was of Min-jah kissing my hand, my phone dings again.

Who is this? 😺

Standing there trembling my mind goes blank when a sudden knock on my door startled me. I rushed to the door and then slowly reached out my hand to grab the door handle. The handle rattles slightly as my hand trembles slowly turning the handle. I swing the door open quickly to see Min-jah standing there shocked. Seeing him a flood of relief surged through me immediately making me tear up as I threw myself into his arms. Taken aback by my sudden hug Min-jah chuckles as he gently hugs me back.

"Wait... What's wrong? Why are you trembling?" Min-jah asks distressingly.

Still trembling I hug him even tighter and bury my face into his chest as he rubs the back of my head to soothe me.

I sit at the small table in my kitchen as Min-jah slowly hands me a warm glass of water. Having handed over the glass Min-jah quickly pulls up another chair to sit in front of me. I slowly sip the water for several seconds while he looks at me concerned. I carefully placed the glass on the edge of the table and looked over at Min-jah pitifully.

"What happened?" he finally asks.

I sighed as I slowly handed over my phone and as if I did something wrong I quickly avoided his eyes. Min-jah quietly goes through all the messages I have received. With a furious expression his eyes quickly flashed toward mine. Unsettled I instantly looked away from him.

"Why didn't you tell me?" he snaps.

"It wasn't that serious..." I softly explained.

"Not that serious?!" he hollers unconvinced.

Flinching as the anger in his voice became more intense.

"At the time..." I said softer.

Fuming with anger Min-jah stands up and starts to pace.

"I'm sorry..." I whimper.

"I-I'm not mad at you." he says in a forced gentler tone.

"But there's more..." I said on the verge of tears.

"There's more?" he says, trying to hide his anger.

"I had a dream last night... of my death I think." I said defeatedly. "I sometimes have this recurring dream. It's no big deal usually it's always the same but last night it was different. I could walk normally at first but then my body suddenly felt so heavy like something was stopping me from moving. I couldn't really see where I was but I remember the time was 11:00PM and that you were calling me."

Min-jah sighs heavily as he grabs my hands gently rubbing the rough leather from his gloves against the top of my hands using his thumbs.

"I'll protect you no matter what." he says with a smile.

I smiled softly as his words seemed to sooth my anxiety.

I waved goodbye to Min-jah as he dropped me off in front of the bakery. Still a little scared I took a deep breath before I walked inside. At the end of my shift I met with Yuki-ji to walk her home. I waved goodbye to her as she went inside. I checked the time on my phone, 10:45PM. I carefully looked around before I started to walk back down the street. The time was 10:53PM and my heart started to pound as I walked down the street. My heart nearly leaped right out of my chest as my phone began to ring. I quickly picked it up breathing heavily.

"Hello." I answered breathlessly.

"Where are you?" Min-jah's voice rings in my ear.

"I am walking back from dropping Yuki-ji off at home." I answer with a sigh.

"Okay, from now on I'll call you every night at this time. I'll give you three rings before I will rush to you so you better answer after one." Min-jah commands.

"Okay." I answer as I walk onto the bus.

Getting off the bus I look up to see Min-jah sitting and waiting for me again. I smile when I see him sitting there.

"What are you doing here?" I asked puzzled.

"I was thinking, this person clearly knows where you live." he says "But I'm willing to bet he doesn't know where I live." he smiles as the lights from his car flash.

I smiled as Min-jah urged me to follow him to his car. I placed three folded white shirts, my white sneakers, and a hygiene bag inside a small grey duffle bag. I grabbed my charger quickly. Mr. Snuggles who was sitting in the center of my bed caught my eye. I stared at him for a minute and shook my head deciding I was going to leave him. I picked up the duffle bag and started to head for the door when I stopped dead in my tracks glancing back toward Mr. Snuggles.

I flicked the lights off as I closed and locked the door. Walking down the steps I noticed Mr. Snuggles' leg was hanging out of the bag. I quickly shoved it back in and zipped up the bag. Tossing the bag into the back seat as I got into the car we set out for Min-jah's house.

CHAPTER 8

We pulled up in front of a giant metal gate that appeared to be able to touch the clouds. There was a small beep as Min-jah clicked a button on the key ring. The gate clanked into motion and slowly moved out of the way. He pulled the car through as soon as there was just enough room. At the end of the driveway was a large beautiful white two story house. The front side of the house had ceiling to floor windows that showcased the whole living space from the kitchen to the stairs in the corner leading up to the second story.

On the second story with curtains drawn were large windows easily marking where the main room was. Next to the large windows was an area outside that was lit up with stringed lights. I could see small trees and small pieces of metal that looked like the frame of a swing through the glow of the lights. Min-jah put the car in park and slowly getting out of the car I gazed in amazement. Carrying my bag Min-jah leads the way inside.

"You don't have to worry about anybody, I have a housekeeper who comes in the morning but she will only come in the afternoon during the week now." Min-jah says as we enter the house.

There was an elegant glow radiating from everything inside the house afraid to touch anything I held my hands behind my back. In the kitchen all the cupboards and countertops were a beautiful solid white marble that was accented by the stainless steel appliances including the pots and pans that hung under the cupboards. In the living room the color choice continued as it was neatly decorated with white furniture including the coffee table in the center. There were small house plants littered about as if they were strategically placed that helped break up and add a little color to the room. The stairway leading to the second story was the darkest colored thing on the floor from the black metal hardware holding it together to the deep dark brown mahogany wood steps.

"I'll show you to your room." Min-jah says while walking up the stairs.

He opens up a white door to a large room decorated much like the living room. Located on a navy blue painted wall was the bed with a bedspread to match. Next to the bedside table was a door left slightly ajar that led to the ensuite bathroom. On the other side of the room the wall had been built with a built in shelving filled with a few books, small figurines, and succulent plants acting like bookends. Beside the shelf were two large mirrors that slide open to reveal the closet. I cautiously walked inside as I carefully looked around the room. Min-jah chuckles as he swiftly follows me in placing my bag on the bed.

"Make yourself at home." Min-jah says as he watches me gaze at everything.

"Ha." I scoff.

"I'll make us something to eat so just make yourself comfortable." Min-jah says as he closes the door behind him.

I looked around one last time before I began to unpack my bag. I removed Mr. Snuggles from his small enclosure and mouthed an apology as I smoothed out his fur. Giving him a quick kiss on his forehead I placed him gently in the center of the pillows introducing him to his new throne.

Min-jah rushes down the stairs and into the kitchen so fast he loses his slippers. He excitedly opens the fridge to find it was empty not including a few water bottles in the door. He begins to frantically check the cupboards only to find them in an even worse state. Checking the last cupboard Min-jah crakes a triumphant smile as he finds three packs of ramen. Hanging up my clothes when a soft knock came from the door causing me to glance over as the door slowly creaked open.

"Dinner's ready." Min-jah said softly as he poked his head around the door.

I nodded with a smile as I quickly hung up the last of my clothes. I flew down the stairs and hurriedly placed my sneakers next to Min-jah's shoes by the door before going to the kitchen.

"I don't normally eat at home." Min-jah chuckles nervously as he places the pot of ramen on the table.

I smile as I sit down. Min-jah places two water bottles on the table before sitting down. I grab a bowl and begin to scoop out some noodles and hand it over to Min-jah. He smiles warmly as he carefully takes the bowl out of my hand.

"I'm surprised you even know how to cook this." I joked as I took the first satisfying bite.

"Aside from poorly made scrambled eggs, this is the only thing I know how to cook." Min-jah answers as he fills his mouth.

I snort as I chase a drop of broth running down my chin. Min-jah chuckles as he continues to eat. I was washing the dishes when a pair of covered arms wraps around me from behind. With a startled gasp I wiggled free from the sudden embrace. Wearing a face mask, long sleeves, a pair of gloves, and pants Min-jah held up his hands apologetically as I quickly turned to face him.

"Sorry figured if I was covered it would be okay." he mumbled softly showing how he was wearing gloves and a long sleeve shirt.

I let out a sigh as I instantly regretted my reaction.

"No, I'm sorry. I'm just not used to it." I apologized, grabbing his hands.

I smiled up at him as sweetly as I could until I could tell he had accepted my apology. I wrapped his arms around me as I went back to doing the dishes. He rested his chin on the top of my head as he stood quietly holding me tightly.

"I don't work tomorrow so I can go grocery shopping while you are at work." I state as I leaned my head back on his shoulder to look up at him.

"No, I'll have someone pick up some stuff in the morning. I don't want you going anywhere unless you have to. Not while that creep is out there." he said sternly.

I nodded in agreement as he held me tighter.

Laying on the couch with Joon fast asleep on his chest Min-jah's phone began to ring loudly. Carefully sliding out from underneath his head as not to wake him Min-jah swiftly answers his phone.

"Hello?" he whispers.

"I need you to come into the office immediately. It's important." Byung-woo's voice pleads through the phone.

Min-jah looks over at the peacefully sleeping Joon and sighs with disappointment.

"Alright I'll be right there." he answers softly.

Right before he leaves he covers Joon with a blanket and softly kisses his forehead while still wearing the face mask.

"I'll be right back." he whispers gently as he strokes his hair.

Min-jah walks outside to see a car already waiting for him, the driver opens the back passenger side door as he walks over. The door closes softly behind him with a stern cold look he removes the face mask and nods toward the driver. Arriving at the company Min-jah is greeted by Byung-woo who swiftly escorts him inside.

"While looking into who might be poisoning you I found someone suspicious." Byung-woo explains as they briskly walked across the lobby.

Byung-woo presses the elevator button for the lobby three times quickly and then scans his right thumb print as a finger scanner suddenly appears out of the wall. The doors close and the elevator goes down opening up to a long hallway lit up by fluorescent lights. Byung-woo opens the door to an underground interrogation room located on a secret floor under the employee parking lot. Sitting under a bright light was the employee who was in charge of taking everyone's lunch orders. Squinting as they entered the room the employee's face showed a visible sign of shock as Min-jah walked into the room. Taking his place across from the suspect Min-jah sits down glaring at him.

"W-where am I?" he nervously asks as Byung-woo walks around him.

"Who do you work for?" Byung-woo asks slamming his hand on the table.

"W-what?" he flinches.

"Who do you work for?" Byung-woo repeats harshly.

Confused, he slowly points a shaky finger over at Min-jah. Min-jah squints at him as he leans back in the chair, crossing his arms.

"Then why would you try to kill him?" Byung-woo snaps as he tosses papers on the table.

"WHAT?!" he shouts. "K-KILL?" he stands up defensively as he begins to panic.

"We found your stash of arsenic in your car and your house!" Byung-woo states as he forces him to sit back down.

"A-Ars-!! No there's no way I would have that!" he protests loudly.

"We already had it confirmed." Byung-woo says tapping on the table

Frantic he grabs the papers and starts to read them. Trembling as he places the papers down and looks up at Min-jah desperately.

"I-I I swear I didn't!" he pleads.

"You could have easily done it. Why should we believe you?" Byung-woo questions as he continues walking around the room.

"I-I don't even know what you order is because it always changes." he argues.

"How do you know it always changes?" Byung-woo says speculatively.

"E-E-Everyone knows that it's for s-security purposes!" he says quickly as he nervously fwips his head back and forth between them.

"Sure... but I'm sure that makes it pretty easy to figure out which food order will end up in front of the Chairman, doesn't it?" Byung-woo says accusatively as he passes behind him.

"NO!" he shouts defensively.

"Seems pretty logical to me." Byung-woo shrugs.

"I swear I didn't. I wouldn't." he pleads to Min-jah desperately on the verge of tears.

"If you didn't then point me in the right direction." Min-jah finally says looking at him.

His eyes swell with tears as he stares at Min-jah and begins to sob as he doesn't have an answer for him. Byung-woo nods his head and a security team swiftly comes in and escorts the sobbing man out. Min-jah sighs heavily as he enters the elevator with Byung-woo.

"He didn't do this alone, someone helped him." Min-jah states.

"I'll find him." Byung-woo says determinedly.

"Good. Oh I have another task for you." Min-jah says as the elevator doors open up to the lobby.

"And what's that?" Byung-woo asks puzzled.

"Grocery shopping. Drop it off before seven tomorrow morning." Min-jah demands as he walks away.

"G-grocery shopping?" Byung-woo repeats frazzled as the elevator doors close on him.

I woke up to find I was laying on the couch alone and Min-jah was gone. Looking around I saw the gloves he had been wearing and I gently touched my forehead. A faint memory of Min-jah kissing my forehead flashes in my head I blush as a smile spreads across my face. Wondering where he must have gone I went upstairs to look for him. I slowly opened his bedroom door disappointed he wasn't there.

His room was much larger than mine as he had a whole office set up including multiple computers on a large black desk. There was a large television with a large black leather couch with a small black glass table sitting in front of it. His bed, with a matching bedspread, was located on the back wall that was painted a dark burgundy color. Farther down the same wall was the door to the closet. Followed by a large empty section with a door on the far end that appeared to lead to the outside space. Separating the sections of the room were wooden square open view shelves that stretched all the way to the ceiling.

Besides the ordinary things like books and succulent plants one particular thing on the closest shelf caught my attention. I slowly lifted my hands toward the soft white teddy bear sitting in one of the cubby holes of the shelf. The bear looked just like Mr. Snuggles all the way down to the brown sweater with the heart it was wearing. I smile softly as the memory of the day ten years ago when I first brought Mr. Snuggles home.

A scrawny boy not wearing nearly warm enough clothes stomps repeatedly to knock the snow off his feet before he goes inside a large building. Shoving a beanie inside his coat pocket as he hangs it up he pulls down his shirt sleeves as he walks inside.

"I fixed the boiler." he mumbled with a dirty face.

"Thank you Joon." the head lady says as she dries her hands on her apron.

"I accidentally ripped my gloves again." the thirteen year old Joon says quietly with his head down as he holds up his hands to show holes in both palms.

Annoyed, the head lady grabs a large white envelope out of her apron pocket and takes out a few bills and tosses them in his direction.

"Here, your payment for last month's chores. Hurry and get some new ones before you scare everyone." she scowls.

"Yes ma'am." he answers obediently as he slowly picks up the money.

Laying alone in a room filled with beds, young Joon flips through a book stopping when he comes across a certain page. Lightly running the tip of his finger across a picture of a small blonde girl who was smiling brightly. Tracing her smile with his finger he slowly traced until his finger was over the teddy bear the little girl was holding. Staring intensely young Joon slams the book closed as he rolls over pulling the dirty blanket tightly around him.

Standing in front of a large display window of a toy store was a set of opposite matching teddy bears wearing sweaters. Young Joon glances down at the money in his hand and then back up at the bears. He cautiously walks inside slowly pulling up his tattered hood and sneaks over to the shelf where the bears are at. The shop owner silently creeps up behind the skinny young boy who was standing there staring at the teddy bears.

"If you buy one I won't tell anyone. Promise." the shopkeeper says out of nowhere.

"EEP!" a frightened young Joon slips out as he flinches.

"I'm so sorry." the shopkeeper laughs. "Would you like one?"

Young Joon shyly bowed his head before he nods softly in agreement.

"Well unfortunately the white one already has an owner on their way to come pick it up, but the brown one is still looking for its forever home." the shopkeeper says with a light smile.

At the checkout counter young Joon slowly opens his hand to show the crumpled bills nervously he places them on the glass not looking up. The shopkeeper looked at the almost ₩12,000 that had been placed on the counter and looked at the total of ₩37,000.

"Look at that just enough." he says with a smile as he pops open the register.

Young Joon slowly reaches and picks up the teddy bear running his fingers through the fur with a smile. He waves goodbye to the shopkeeper hugging the teddy bear as he leaves.

Hearing the front door open snaps me back to the present from memory lane. I quickly place the bear back in its spot and dash out the door. Min-jah tosses his keys on the table as he walks into the living room to find Joon wasn't on the couch. I pattered down the stairs quickly to find Min-jah wearing a suit standing in the living room.

"Where did you go so late?" I asked as I finished coming down the stairs.

"Had something at the office I had to take care of, are you ready for bed?" Min-jah asks with a smile.

"Mmm" I answered with a smile.

I laid there staring up at the ceiling, unable to fall asleep I rolled over and looked at the door. Tossing off the blanket I got up and made my way towards the door. The door creaked open as I slowly peeked out and looked down the darkened hallways towards Min-jah's bedroom door. Slipping out of the room I quietly closed the door behind me. Mr. Snuggles in hand I silently snuck down the hall until I was right in front of Min-jah's door. I took a deep breath and slowly released it as I raised my hand and softly knocked on the door.

Tossing the corner of the blanket aside, Min-jah sits up with a sigh and turns to look as a soft knock comes from the door. I nervously waited for him to open the door hoping he had not already fallen asleep. I went to walk away when the door suddenly opened. Nervous I instantly brought up Mr. Snuggles and hid my mouth behind his head.

"C-can I sleep in here with you..." I softly stuttered as I looked up at him from behind Mr. Snuggles's head.

Min-jah stared at me silently with an expression I was unfamiliar with until he smiled softly and let me in.

Min-jah changed into pajama pants, a long sleeve shirt, put on his leather gloves, and a pair of socks before he crawled into bed next to me.

"This is inconvenient isn't it?" I asked softly, a little guilty.

"Not at all." He answered with a smile before he put on a face mask.

"I'll just go back to my room." I say unconvinced as I go to crawl out of bed.

Min-jah grabs my arm and pulls me down into his arms placing my head on his chest. He covers me with the blanket as he pulls me closer to him by my waist.

"Go to sleep." He demands as he strokes my hair lightly.

I closed my eyes with a smile as I snuggled deeper into his body. As I was about to fall asleep I heard Min-jah suddenly calling my name.

"Joon... Joon are you asleep?" Min-jah asks in a whisper.

"Hmm?" I answer sleepily.

"I have a question." he says.

"Hmm?" I repeat.

"Why do you use your ability to save people?" he asks quietly.

Surprised at the sudden serious question I looked up at him with one eye open.

"I think I decided to ten years ago." I answered with a yawn.

"Why?" He asked with an inquisitive tone.

I sat up to chase away my sleepiness and grabbed Mr. Snuggles. I stroked his fur slowly as Min-jah sat up behind me.

"Ten years ago on a particularly cold winter day I was supposed to be out buying new gloves but I decided to buy this bear instead... I was genuinely incredibly happy for the first time when I brought it home. I wasn't paying attention to where I was walking on my way back and I bumped into this boy knocking him down into the snow. I felt terrible about running into him plus I simply thought there's no way this kid wouldn't be wearing gloves because of how cold it was so I offered to help him up. But much to my surprise he wasn't wearing gloves and before I could react he already grabbed my hand and pulled himself up. At that moment when I saw how he was going to die I felt a kind of sadness I'd never felt before. It felt like my heart was literally breaking, scared of what I was feeling I ran away. I probably made it about a block or two away when something inside me made me turn around. For some reason I desperately wanted this boy to live so I started running fast, back to the boy. I grabbed the hood of his coat and pulled him backwards as hard as I could seconds before this giant neon sign could crush him. While laying in the snow four large men in black suits surrounded him I panicked and snuck away before he could even stand up. I don't remember what that boy's face looked like anymore but every time I look at Mr. Snuggles I am reminded of him and that I could actually save people. After that I worked really hard at trying to save people whose death was preventable." I said nostalgically.

I looked up to see Min-jah had gotten out of bed and was standing by the shelf that held the matching teddy bear to Mr. Snuggles. He picks up the bear and smiles as he turns toward me.

"When I was thirteen after being miraculously saved from a sign that was going to crush me by a stranger I passed by the toy store that was up the street and saw this bear. It looked similar to the bear the boy was holding in his hand, I got this strange compulsion that I needed this toy and at that very moment. I rushed into the store telling the owner I wanted to buy it but he refused saying someone had already bought it. Frustrated and honestly terrified that I might lose it I offered to pay triple the amount it was worth. Uncertain that I had that kind of money on me he still wouldn't sell it to me but told me if I could come back in twenty minutes with the money he would give it to me. I ran to the closest ATM I could find and pulled out as much money as it would give me. I made it back to the store with three minutes left. That was the first time in my life I ever felt genuinely happy to be born to a rich family." Min-jah discloses as he looks at me affectionately.

Left completely speechless I stared at Min-jah as he made his way to the side of the bed. I looked up at him with teary eyes as he stood beside me. He slowly raised his hands up and gently wiped the tear that had escaped rolling down my cheek. He placed his knee on the edge of the bed next to me as he slowly caressed my face. Leaning in closer he stopped just inches before our foreheads would touch.

The face mask being the only barrier between us he gently touches his nose to mine. I close my eyes as the heat from his breath seeps through the mask and warms my skin. He places a hand on the back of my neck and slowly guides me down on the bed. Breathing heavily, I opened my eyes desperately wanting to feel more than the heat from his breath. He firmly presses his lips against my forehead through the mask before he gets up leaving me lying on the bed.

"I'm going to go lay on the couch until I can trust myself to behave." Min-jah says with a blanket and pillow already in hand.

Still staring up at the ceiling, I slowly nodded my head as he walked into the other section of the room. With my heart still racing and my face flushed I sat up and got into bed properly.

"G-good night." I stuttered out quickly as I turned out the lights.

"Good night." he replies.

CHAPTER 9

Sitting on the couch in the living room sipping on a cup of coffee while watching the sun rise I heard the door unlock. As I quickly rounded the corner I saw a man with his arms loaded with a dozen or more grocery bags. He struggles to turn around in the entryway to close the door. Finally managing to close the door using his foot he proceeds to enter the house tripping over my white sneakers.

"Whose shoes-" he stops as he looks up and sees me standing there.

He quickly looks around as if to double check and make sure he didn't walk into someone else's house by accident.

"Who are you?" he finally asks with a bewildered expression.

"Ah right on time. I'm starving." Min-jah suddenly says coming down the stairs still wearing the gloves and face mask.

We both quickly looked over at him as he smiled and waved for the man to go to the kitchen.

"Why are you wearing gloves and a mask?" the man asks perplexed.

I sat awkwardly at the kitchen table while the man slowly put away the groceries staring at me. Min-jah sits down next to me drinking a cup of coffee with the face mask nestled under his chin.

"Let me introduce you to my best friend and the only person whom I trust with the hassles of my everyday life Kim Byung-woo." he says with a confident smile as he points to the man unloading the groceries.

I grinned shyly and nodded my head as he continued to stare at me. I awkwardly looked away and continued to drink my coffee.

"Byung-woo, this is Park-Chul Joon. Due to some unavoidable circumstances he will be living here with me from now on." Min-jah explains nonchalantly.

I choked on my coffee as a loud clatter came from Byung-woo who dropped a can.

"He's what?" Byung-woo shouts rushing around the counter to the table. "Just who is he?" he says as he points at me.

I instinctively hid behind the coffee cup trying to avoid his angry gaze.

"He is my boyfriend." Min-jah answered casually as he continued to drink his coffee.

My face instantly turned a bright red as Byung-woo dropped his jaw and stared at Min-jah in complete disbelief.

"Min-jah, what are you talking about?!" I whispered embarrassed as I hid behind my coffee cup again.

I stood in the kitchen making breakfast as Min-jah and Byung-woo sat in the living room talking. Stealing little glances at them concerned my eyes accidently met Byung-woo's as I stole another glance. I quickly turned away embarrassed and continued to make breakfast.

"So you're telling me the random pâtissier you had me look into saved your life that night and he is also the kid who saved you ten years ago from that sign?" Byung-woo asks, astonished while looking back at Min-jah.

"That's right." Min-jah explains excitedly.

"Interesting…" Byung-woo says sarcastically. "Now how did he end up living here?"

"He has a stalker." Min-jah answers coldly.

"Okay, what about just informing the police?" Byung-woo asks.

"No." Min-jah answers sharply.

"Mmkay." Byung-woo says concerned. "What's with the get up though?" he asks, hoping to turn the conversation.

"Oh." Min-jah looked down at his hands, "It's nothing." he answered hesitantly.

"Is he really your boyfriend?" Byung-woo says glancing toward Joon.

"Are you even listening to me?" Min-jah protests.

"Well he seemed just as shocked as me to hear that." Byung-woo points out.

Min-jah looks at him with a grin and shrugs his shoulders as he glances over at the kitchen. Seeing how Min-jah's face softened Byung-woo frowns as he gets stonewalled with every question.

"Um b-breakfast is ready." I say softly from the kitchen.

I ate slowly as I waited for their reactions as they started to eat.

"Whoa this is delicious." Byung-woo says pleasantly surprised.

Min-jah squeezes my hand softly under the table making me smile as we continue to eat. I sat across the table from a glaring Byung-woo as Min-jah did the dishes in the kitchen. I looked over at Min-jah anxiously who smiled back at me softly. I look back at Byung-woo who was still looking at me with his eyes narrowed.

"Well I'm happy to meet you." Byung-woo finally says happily as he extends his hand out.

I looked at his hand nervously when Min-jah, with his hands back in his gloves, suddenly pulled me into a hug. One hand holding my wrists and the other on the side of my head squeezing me lightly. Surprised by his reaction Byung-woo stared up at Min-jah with a curious smile.

"No touching." Min-jah says playfully.

"Okay, okay." Byung-woo says tossing his hands up in surrender.

I stood in the entryway as Min-jah and Byung-woo put their shoes on to leave.

"I'll be back tonight." Min-jah says as he gently strokes my cheek.

I smile softly as I sink my chin into the rough leather of his gloves hoping he would decide to stay.

"Ew. Alright enough PDA let's go you are already late." Byung-woo says to urge Min-jah out the door.

The house suddenly felt very empty as I waved goodbye and the door closed. Not sure what to do with the rest of the day, I slowly walked back upstairs.

Sitting in a room full of clay pots, Mama Tookie was quietly spinning a lump of clay. Carefully she glides her hands across the clay as she forms the shape of a jar. She forms the lip of the jar as she gracefully smoothes out the sides. Stopping the wheel she takes a wire and quickly slides it underneath the freshly made jar. Slowly standing up she walks over to a shelf where she moves around some other clay projects to make room for her new one. She slowly and carefully picks up the new jar to transfer it to its new home. While walking back toward the shelf suddenly startled she drops the still wet clay jar. The jar squashes against the floor as she braces herself against the shelf as she struggles to breathe. Mizuki darts into the room running up to her meowing loudly.

"Mizuki I'm going to need you to run an errand for me." Mama Tookie says breathlessly.

Laying in Min-jah's bed I stared up at the ceiling as I sighed from boredom. I rolled over to face Mr. Snuggles reaching up, I started stroking his fur as my phone started to ring. I looked at the screen and began to tremble slightly as it was from an unknown number.

"H-hello?" I answered hesitantly.

"Waaaaa!!" comes a loud familiar whine through the phone.

"Yuki-ji?" I say rubbing my ear.

"Why aren't you at home!!" she whines again.

"Oh." I say as I look around the room.

"Whatever it's not important I need you to come home immediately." she cries.

"Why? What's wrong?" I ask as I start to walk around the room.

"You remember that birthday present I bought for my sister several months ago? And I had you keep it at your place?" she asks impatiently.

"Uhh yeah?" I answer not actually remembering.

"Well today's her birthday and I need it so I can catch the train. So please come home quickly." she pleads.

"Okay, okay I'll be right there." I say.

I arrive at home to find Yuki-ji standing in front of my door panicking. I shake my head as I head up the stairs.

"Finally!" she shouts when she sees me.

"Sorry." I apologized as I pulled up the screen covering the keypad.

"Hurry, hurry." she impatiently whispers.

I open the door as she rushes past me inside I shook my head as I followed her in. I close the door behind us as she frantically looks around for the present. I walked inside and noticed the present was sitting on top of my desk. I hold it up for her to see, with a bright smile she snatches it out of my hand.

"Thank you thank you thank you." she repeats as we walk out the door.

"It's nothing." I laugh as I turn to lock my door.

"I'll see you at work!" she says as she rushes off.

I chuckle as I hear the click of the door locking. I turned around to see Mizuki standing at the top of the stairway.

"Mizuki?" I question.

He meows in reply and then turns to walk down the stairs, turning back to see if I was following him. Perplexed, I followed him all the way to Mama Tookie's shop. I pushed open the door slowly letting Mizuki inside.

"Mama Tookie?" I said apprehensively as I walked through the shop.

Mizuki meowed again before he walked down the hallway that led to where Mama Tookie stayed. I pushed the curtain aside and followed him down the hall. Sitting at her dining room table, Mama Tookie nervously chewed on her thumb nail.

"Mama Tookie?" I ask concerned.

"Ah the bestowed!" she hollers happily as she wraps me in a hug.

Noticing that it was only me she frowned as she turned to Mizuki.

"Mizuki! Where is the bonded?" she hollers.

Mizuki meows sharply and then darts into the other room. Confused I look at Mama Tookie as she shakes her head annoyed.

"What's the matter Mama Tookie?" I ask.

She looked at me distressingly as she squeezed my arm. I looked at her with concern as her grip tightened.

Mama Tookie sets a cup of tea on the table in front of me before sitting down herself.

"Let me see the crystal." she demands.

Puzzled, I pull the crystal necklace out from under my shirt. The crystal was now three quarters of the way mixed with the dark green color. Surprised I looked up at Mama Tookie who was anything but pleased.

"Just what I was afraid of." Mama Tookie says with a hint of irritation.

"What do you mean?" I ask.

"I said a bond cannot be rushed but the bestowed rushed it anyways." she scolded.

"What? I haven't rushed anything." I argued.

"Then explain this!" she hissed as she grabbed the crystal.

"I-I don't know the last time I looked at it was the day you gave it to me and only the tip was green!" I said defensively.

"Then the bonded?" she quickly snaps back.

"No he hasn't done anything either! Just what is going on?!" I hollered in frustration.

"The bond is getting too strong too fast. The ill-fated will feel it too." she mumbles.

"Ill-fated?" I repeat.

"Ah the bonded knows." Mama Tookie says while tossing up her hands in frustration.

"Wait!" I say following her as she leaves the room.

"Tell the bonded that it could happen soon to be ready." Mama Tookie warns

"What are you talking about?!" I ask.

"Just tell the bonded, it already knows everything." she insists.

Exhausted from asking questions and not having them answered I sigh as she continues to mumble cryptic things to herself.

"Everything is happening too fast. Too young to have a bonded. Too young when decided. Too fast. Too fast." she mumbles.

Walking away I looked back at her pacing as if trying to figure out a problem. I shook my head as I left the shop.

"Bestowed!" she hollers after me.

"What?" I answer harshly as she rushes to catch up.

"The reason the bond is growing so fast is because the bestowed is too strong. When the bestowed decided how to use the gift at such a young age the gift evolved. The bestowed still needs a bonded to control the gift but the bond could have been formed much sooner than usual." she explains calmly.

We walked back to her shop as she insisted she had more to tell me. We sat at her kitchen table as she went over everything she had already told Min-jah.

"So because of the way I have decided to use this ability, I will make it harder on Min-jah?" I asked to confirm.

"Because the bestowed decided that path there will be many ill-fated some having a stronger urge than others but ill-fated nevertheless the bonded must handle all of them." Mama Tookie explains.

"Can't I just decide again?" I suggest.

"No." she snapped, "Once a decision has been made it can't be undone without consequences."

"Consequences? Like what?" I pried.

"If the bestowed changes the decision now then the original decision will need to be undone. To do so every decision the bestowed has made using the gift since then will too." she explains thoughtfully.

"So every person I have saved since I was thirteen will die." I say as I understand.

"Including the bonded. Since this action was the catallus for the decision." she adds mournfully.

I sat on the bus staring off into space as I thought about what Mama Tookie had said. I closed my eyes tightly and clenched my fists. Thinking back to all the times I used this ability to save someone I knew I could never change my decision. I opened my eyes slowly knowing that my choice could only make Min-jah suffer.

Slamming down a stack of binders on the desk Byung-woo flinches as he looks up.

"Byung-wooooo." Seon whines.

"What?" Byung-woo whines back.

"He's refusing to work. He won't take any of the documents from me. Help please..." she cries.

"Okay, I'll take care of it." Byung-woo sighs.

Min-jah lets out a huge exaggerated sigh as Byung-woo comes into his office.

"Again with the sighing?" Byung-woo says as he walks over. "He's waiting for you at home so why are you being like this?" he says pushing a pile of binders closer to Min-jah.

Min-jah begins to pout as he pushes his chair away from the desk and slowly starts spinning in circles. Byung-woo rolls his eyes at the childish Min-jah who started to groan while spinning.

"Come on-" Byung-woo tries.

"Uuuuuugh." Min-jah groans interrupting him.

"Just-" Byung-woo tries again.

"Uuuuuuuugh." Min-jah groans again but louder.

"Okay fine." Byung-woo spits out in irritation.

Min-jah stops spinning and peaks over at Byung-woo from around the edge of his chair.

"If you can get all the important documents done by..." he checks his watch, "two o' clock, you can leave. How about that?" Byung-woo compromises.

With a smile on his face, Min-jah quickly pulls back up to his desk and immediately gets to work. Byung-woo sighs and shakes his head as he gets up and walks out.

"Is he going to work now?" Seon asks as she receives a phone call.

Byung-woo nods with a thumbs up as her face lights up hearing Min-jah on the line requesting all the rejected documents. Exhausted already Byung-woo sits back down at his desk with a sigh. A phone suddenly starts ringing annoyed he pulls out his cell phone to find it wasn't ringing. The ringing continues as Byung-woo opens a drawer to his desk that had multiple phones in it. Reaching in he pulls out the phone that was ringing with a cold expression on his face he answers it.

Min-jah sighs in content as he signs the last important document. Setting down his pen next to the stack of binders he checked the time. He grinned ear to ear he excitedly gathered up his things and prepared to leave. Walking out all the closest employees that were sitting down stood up and bowed. Fixing his jacket he looked up at Seon who was walking toward him with more binders.

"Seon I'm heading out for the rest of the day just leave those on my desk." Min-jah says with a smile as he quickly passes by her.

"Ah wait..." she said disheartedly as he was already gone.

Hong-gi stands in the window looking down at Min-jah as he quickly leaves the building. With a disgruntled groan he walks back over to his desk and pulls out his phone.

"Where is he going?" he growls.

"Home sir." comes a soft male voice.

"Have you figured out more about his visit to the doctor?" he asks.

"Yes, sir. He was diagnosed with acute arsenic poisoning." the voice answered.

He sat there with the phone up to his ear in silence.

"The situation has already been completely handled by Kim Byung-woo sir." the voice says sheepishly.

Angered by the mere mention of that name Hong-gi immediately hangs up the phone and tosses it on his desk. He angrily grunts and mumbles under his breath as he nervously bites his thumb nail.

Min-jah rushes inside excitedly as soon as he closes his car door. Once inside he notices that Joon was nowhere to be seen he glances at the row of shoes in front of the door. With both pairs of Joon's shoes still there he gets a worrisome feeling as he quickly rushes up the stairs. He pushes open the door to the room Joon is staying in to find it empty. As the feeling grows he runs down the hall to his room. He flings open the door to find Joon laying on his bed asleep with his teddy bear. He sighs a breath of relief as he walks up to the sleeping Joon. Smiling he reaches down and lightly strokes Joon's cheek. I wake up with a soft groan to something rough rubbing against my cheek.

"I'm sorry I didn't mean to wake you." Min-jah says in a soft voice.

"That's okay." I say with a smile as I stretch. "Oh, I have something to tell you."

Confused, Min-jah raises his eyebrows as I sit up in bed. I then began to tell him everything that Mama Tookie and I talked about. Including what would happen if I decided not to use my ability to help people. We sat opposite each other on the bed in silence as I finished telling him.

"I won't change the way I'm using this ability. I can't." I say firmly.

Min-jah smiles "I know."

"I don't want to make it harder on you." I continue to babble.

"I know." Min-jah answers as he scoots closer to me.

"I just couldn't handle it knowing I could have changed the outcome." I say as if the person I was trying to convince was myself and not Min-jah.

"I know." Min-jah grabs my hand softly, "I will protect you from all the ill-fated bonds you create."

I smiled gently as I looked up at him and saw there was no hint of him being worried in the slightest over my decision.

"I want to try something." I say breaking the silence.

"What?" he asks.

"I have to prove to myself just how strong I really am." I say determined as I pulled his glove off his hand.

"Are you sure about this?" he questions.

I nod firmly as I stare at him.

"Okay." he agrees.

Min-jah takes off his other glove and holds out his hands palm facing me. Staring at his hands I gulped as I slowly raised my hands. I flattened out my palms shakily as my heart started to race. Trembling I closed my eyes tightly as I slowly moved my hands forward until our hands touched. I gasped opening my eyes with a smile as I grabbed his hands tighter. Smiling Min-jah squeezes my hands back.

"I can't believe it." I say softly as I intertwined my fingers with his.

"Well Mama Tookie did say you were much stronger than any bestowed before you." Min-jah says mockingly.

I chuckle softly as I rubbed my thumb against the top of his hand. Min-jah pulls me in closer for a quick hug before he stands up.

"I thought of a pet name for you." Min-jah says stroking my hair.

"A pet name?" I ask looking up at him.

"Yeah. A name that only I can call you." he explains.

"Okay, what is it?" I asked intrigued.

"Joonie-ah." he says in a cute little voice with a smile.

Pressing my lips together tightly I try to hide the huge smile that wanted to spread across my face.

"Okay, then I'll call you…" I trail off as I thought. "Min Min." I finally say with a laugh looking up at him.

His cheeks instantly turn a bright shade of red as the name slips out of my mouth. Embarrassed, he chuckles as he shakes his head and walks away from me. Covering my eyes Min-jah walks into the bathroom after taking off his shirt. Walking out of the bathroom in a white tank top and dark basketball shorts Min-jah lays down in the bed.

"I took the rest of the day off so let's take a nap." he says as he closes his eyes and smiles.

"Mmm." I agree as I lay my head against his chest.

Walking out of his office Byung-woo makes his way down the wall to check up on Min-jah.

"He's already gone." Seon says distractedly while looking at her computer.

"He's what? Gone?" Byung-woo asks as he stops in his tracks.

"Yep left about an hour ago." she answers while rapidly clicking her mouse.

"He actually finished?" Byung-woo mumbles to himself.

"What?" Seon asks.

"Are all the important documents taken care of?" he asks.

"Yep. Just got done filing all of them. He took off before the ink dried on the last one." she chuckled while clicking her mouse again.

"Perfect." Byung-woo chuckles.

"Huh?" she questions.

"Nothing." Byung-woo answers with a smile as he raps his knuckles on her desk.

A tall buff man with an expressionless face and a buzz cut stands at attention in front of Hong-gi's desk. Staring at him with a disapproving frown, Hong-gi suddenly throws his shoe at the man who doesn't even flinch as it flies right past his face.

"I'm sorry sir." he says as he bows his head.

"How could you let this happen?" Hong-gi shouts angrily.

"I apologize I should have caught on quicker as head of security." he says with his head still bowed.

"We can't let him weasel his way out again, we have to get this right." Hong-gi spits out angrily.

"I understand." he says, picking up his head.

"Get out." Hong-gi growls.

The large man walks out of the office almost running into a smaller skinner man with flat black hair and wearing glasses who was waiting right outside the door.

"KI-HA!" Hong-gi shouts.

Flinching the scrawnier male rushes into the office.

"Yes Director Lan." Ki-ha says with a bow.

"Like you were saying over the phone, tell me how Kim Byung-woo handled the arsenic situation?" Hong-gi asks while looking out the large windows on the other side of the office.

"Yes sir." Ki-ha answered as a smile crept across his face.

CHAPTER 10

Quiet tapping echoes through the silent house as Min-jah sits on the living room floor. Laying behind him on the couch I yawn softly as I stared at the muscles in his neck twitching as he types away. I glance up as the sun slowly creeps over the horizon as light begins to flood the room. Drawing my attention I slowly moved my hand toward the back of his head. Hesitantly I began to push my fingers through his surprisingly soft hair. Surprised Min-jah stops typing and leans his head into the soothing touch of my fingertips.

"Enjoying yourself?" Min-jah asks with a chuckle as he continues to type.

"Mmm." I answer softly.

"Good." Min-jah answers with a smile.

Feeling impulsive I sit up placing my legs on either side of him. I slide my fingers down the side of his neck pulling his chin upwards. Leaning forward I pressed my lips heavily against his. Min-jah closes his eyes as he reaches up and turns my head as he proceeds to kiss me back. Gasping for breath I pull away from him with a smile.

"Min Min… I think I love you…" I say breathlessly as I stare at him.

"Ha…" Min-jah chuckles "I think I love you too Joonie-ah." he says as he pulls me into another kiss.

Min-jah gets out of the black town car with an overly wide smile as he makes his way to the front of the office. Greeted with the usual head bow and occasional 'Good morning Chairman Lan.' as he entered the main lobby. Unprecedentedly he greeted the employees back with a large smile and a 'good morning' as he continued through the building. Sitting at his desk with a giddy smile Min-jah works his way through binder after binder signing the proposals he approved and tossing the others. He places his pen down on his desk leaning back with a sigh and stretching before he reaches up and hits the small black button on the front of his phone.

"Seon." he calls.

Immediately she opens the door and bows as she enters.

"Yes sir?" she says.

"I'm finished with all the proposals if you could file them for me I'd appreciate it." he says with a smile.

Surprised she glances up to find Min-jah sitting back in his chair smiling and giggling to himself. A little intrigued she grabs the stack of binders and turns to leave. Unable to ignore it, she stopped in her tracks turning back around to satisfy her curiosity.

"Sir, did something good happen?" she hypothesizes.

"Huh?" he says as his smile fades away.

"Ah... well it just seems you are in a good mood today. Sir." she blurts out in a panic.

"Hmm." Min-jah chuckles with a smile.

She awkwardly stands there clutching the binders tightly expecting to be scolded.

"Yeah." he finally answers with a smile "Something pretty great happened."

"That's good to hear." she answers breathlessly as she opens the office door.

She carefully closes the door as she lets out a loud exaggerated sigh while placing the binders on her desk. She places her hand over her heart dramatically as she takes deep breaths and rapidly fans her face.

"What happened? Did he scold you?" a concerned employee asks.

"Are the rumors a lie? Is he not in a good mood?" asks another.

She turned her head sharply as she glared at them. Her expression instantly melted as a joyful smile spread across her face.

"You wouldn't believe what I just witnessed." she squeals with delight.

Relieved other employees started to gather around to hear the story. Sitting at a round table in the employee break room, Seon was repeating the morning's events again to yet another group of employees.

"He then chuckled lightly as he looked toward the window with a longing gaze before he finally said 'Yeah, something pretty great happened.' with the softest smile I have ever seen." she exaggerates as she dramatically acts out the scene.

"Awe I would have killed to see that smile." a female employee says with a disappointed sigh.

"I was so sure my heart was going to explode I swooned so hard." Seon explains as she drinks her coffee.

Walking quickly toward the opened break room door Byung-woo heard the lively chatter of the employees intrigued he slowed down as he passed.

"Ah Byung-woo!" Seon shouts as he passes.

Stopping in his tracks, Byung-woo backs up and peaks around the door. Seon urgently waves him over with a mouth full of coffee. Byung-woo flashed a small smile as he entered the break room.

"You have to tell us." Seon says in a rush.

"Tell you?" Byung-woo asks confused.

"Does Chairman Lan have a girlfriend?" she asks quickly.

"Uh…" Byung-woo says as he looks at the faces of all the urging employees. "W-well no he doesn't have a *girl*friend…" he says avoiding their gazes.

Disappointed they all slump in their seats with a sigh.

"Why what's going on?" Bung-woo questions.

"He's in a good mood today and when I asked him about it he seemed to be thinking of someone while smiling." she explains downcastedly.

"Ah he must be thinking about Joon." Byung-woo accidently lets slip out.

"Joon?" the table of employees repeated in shock.

Byung-woo quickly slaps his hand over his mouth as he swiftly runs out of the break room. Stunned the table of employees sat and watched as he quickly made his escape before jumping up and chasing after him. Finally cornering him in his office the employees surrounded Byung-woo.

"Now, now gossiping is highly dangerous behavior." Byung-woo chuckled out nervously as the crowd closed in on him.

"Who is Joon?" Seon asks in a crazed voice.

"W-well he-" Byung-woo stutters as she gets closer.

"He?" she interrupts shocked.

"W-well you asked about a girlfriend... and well it's true he doesn't have one..." Byung-woo explains quickly.

The fury of the employees began to fade as they slowly started to guess what Byung-woo was implying.

"So he has a..." Seon falls silent as the pieces of the puzzle click into place.

"Ah ha..." Byung-woo chuckles lightly as the crowd's mood softens.

With a scatter of mumbling and whispering as the crowd began to slowly digest the gossip and dissipate. Byung-woo shook his head and grinned as he watched the disappointed employees slowly file out and go back to work.

"Ah I hope that doesn't come back to me." Byung-woo says exasperatedly as he slumps in his office chair.

Standing next to the window glancing over with a cold stare as the door clicks open softly as Ki-ha slips in.

"Director Lan." Ki-ha bows.

"What is it?" Hong-gi huffs.

"There are rumors that Chairman Lan is seeing someone." Ki-ha says.

"Is that so?" Hong-gi says intrigued.

"They are saying it's the young man named Joon." Ki-ha says quietly.

"Joon?" Hong-gi repeats, turning to look at Ki-ha.

Ki-ha stands there not saying a word as Hong-gi walks over to him.

"As in that young man who saved Min-jah the night of the inauguration? Hong-gi asks quickly.

"It would appear so Sir." Ki-ha confirms.

"Interesting... very interesting..." Hong-gi says with an unexpected smile on his face.

Min-jah leans against the hood of his car impatiently as he checks the time on his watch. With a sigh he starts to pace the length of the car while staring down the dark road. He checks his watch again and quickly pulls out his phone and makes a call. After one ring the line clicks open.

"I'm on my way back now." I say instantly after answering my phone.

"This is making me a nervous wreck. I wish I could just walk you both instead of waiting at the end of the street." Min-jah complains.

"Don't be silly, you have to work and you work later than both of us. You can't just stop everything just to be able to walk us." I chuckle.

"Nothing is more important than you." Min-jah bluntly says.

"Ha you really are shameless." I blush.

"Only when it comes to you." Min-jah says in a flirty voice.

I roll my eyes and smile when I hear a rustling noise coming from behind me. I stopped and turned around to look down the dark alleyway.

"Hurry up it's cold." Min-jah whines.

"Okay I'm coming." I say distractedly as I turn back around.

I could see Min-jah in the distance leaning against his car while he waited for me and I couldn't hide my smile.

"I can see you so I'm hanging up now." I say as I waved toward him.

"Okay I see you too." he answers as he waves back at me.

I walk up to him with a smile and immediately give him a hug. He hugs me back tightly kissing the top of my head before he leads me to the car. Holding his hand while he drove I looked at him and smiled, squeezing his hand tighter. He quickly glances at me and smiles as he squeezes my hand back.

Min-jah glances down at our hands intertwined together as he turns off the car engine he sits and stares for a few seconds until he slowly lets go. He quickly rushes around the car to open my door immediately holding out his hand again. Smiling at me with a wide goofy grin with his hand extended like a child I laughed as I gave in and grabbed his hand. He held on tightly as we walked to the front door, not letting go, he unlocked the door. He struggles to take off his shoes, still refusing to let go and headed upstairs. Laying in bed still wearing our coats holding hands I rubbed my eyes and yawned as I snuggled closer to his body. Min-jah kissed my forehead as he finally released my hand reluctantly.

"It's late let's get ready for bed Joonie-ah." he says as he gently brushes my hair out of my face.

"Mmm okay Min Min." I agree with a sleepy smile.

I sleepily sunk my nose into the warm strawberry scented bubble bath as Min-jah sat behind me. Gently scrubbing my back he reached over and grabbed the shampoo and started to wash my hair. Sitting there with my eyes closed I melted into the soothing feeling of his fingers scratching my scalp and running through my hair. Struggling to keep my head up as Min-jah gently rinsed my hair. He chuckled softly as I leaned back against him falling asleep.

Wearing a white robe Min-jah carried me out of the bathroom through the closest and set me on the edge of the bed. Coming over with the blow dryer he pointed to the floor. Grinning through my half opened eyes I slipped onto the floor. Leaning my head against his leg I sat on the floor as he carefully blow dried my hair. I closed my eyes as I soaked up the warmth from his fingers running through my hair and from the blow dryer. Running his fingers through my hair one last time making sure it's properly dried I leaned my head back to look up at him.

"I think I love you Min Min." I say through a gentle smile as I closed my eyes.

Grinning as he turns off the dryer, Min-jah lifts my chin higher as he leans down and presses his lips against mine. I lifted my hand placing it on the back of his head and pulled him closer as I slowly shifted to my knees. He slides his hand down my back and lifts me up onto the bed by my waist, our lips never parting. Laying me on my back he pushes his body in between my legs pulling my thighs up to rest on his legs. I wrap my arms around his neck as his right hand finds its home on my hip bone and the other entangled in my hair. Gasping for breath we finally pulled apart. He slowly strokes my cheek as he stares at me.

"I think I love you too Joonie-ah." he says through a smile catching his breath as he leans over gently kissing me again.

Pulling my face away from him I closed my eyes and gasped softly as the hand that was in my hair suddenly gripped tightly and pulled my head back. He slips his hand under the robe as he continues to kiss my neck. I bit my lip moaning softly as a tingling sensation began to course through every part of my body. His lips made a slow trail down my neck leading down to my collar bone. I run my hands down his back pulling his body closer to mine when I start to feel something hard pushing against me. I stopped and looked at him to find his face completely flushed as he looked back at me. Through his gasping breaths I could hear him silently pleading, begging me to let him continue. I grinned as I leaned up kissing him softly to give him the answer he so desperately wanted.

Falling back down my hands above my head as the robe loosely tied folds open. Min-jah lightly bites his bottom lip as his eyes gaze at my body. My heart beats loudly as he reaches up gently stroking my jaw letting his hand slowly and softly trace the side of my neck. Chuckling softly as his hand makes its way through my chest and down toward my navel. I let out a soft moan with a gasp as he continued on his exploration.

Min-jah laid in bed holding Joon tightly as he slept soundly next to him. Gazing down at Joon he reached up and softly shifted the fringe of his bangs softly when Joon's phone rang from the bedside table. Slowly pulling his arm out from under Joon's head Min-jah reached across the bed and grabbed the phone. Unlocking it he finds a text message from an unknown number.

You are surprisingly good at hiding...

Thankfully I'm a master at hide n' seek...

I won't let you touch him.

Oh? Who is this?

I'm the one who will protect him.

Ooo sounds like a fun game...

I dare you to try and lay a finger on him.

I'll kill you myself.

Min-jah sat in the dark, staring at the screen while squeezing the phone tightly as he began to fill with anger.

While cooking breakfast Min-jah walked up and wrapped his arms around me resting his head in the nook of my neck. I chuckled using the hand that was free to pat the top of his head. He hugged me tightly before kissing my neck softly as he let go to go sit down. I smiled sweetly as I watched him drink his coffee and read the morning newspaper. Carefully placing the dishes on the table I smiled when he looked up at me as I poured the juice. As I sat down Min-jah reached his hand across the table I instantly slid my hand into his.

As my hand touched his I gasped as I clenched his hand tightly. I was at an abandoned construction site, I saw several people beating Min-jah with pieces of wood and metal bats. While laying on the ground coughing up blood he is forced to sit up as someone walks out of the shadows. Although I couldn't see this person's face clearly I could feel the pain of Min-jah's heart shattering as this person walks closer to him. Holding a large metal crowbar this person slowly lifts it up before smashing it down onto Min-jah's head. Laying there Min-jah slowly reaches his hand out towards the crystal necklace laying on the ground as a pool of blood begins to flow past his hand. Tears instantly fell down my face as I cried out loud and yanked my hand out of his in a panic and crumbled onto the floor. Breathing heavily, sobbing I grabbed my head and frantically began checking for blood. Min-jah instantly runs to my side reaching his hand out to touch me.

"Don't touch me!" I scream.

He flinches as I have never raised my voice before but he slowly lowers his hand. I close my eyes tightly crying as I hold my aching body rubbing my head. After a while I was finally able to open my eyes as the pain subsided. Sitting behind me wearing pants, a long sleeve shirt, gloves, and the face mask was Min-jah waiting patiently. I instantly began to sob uncontrollably, throwing myself into his arms. He holds me tightly and rubs the back of my head to comfort me as I continue to sob into his chest.

"What did you see?" he finally asks as I calmed down.

"You were at an abandoned construction site, K mall apartments I think? I've never heard of it before." I said trying to remember.

"What happened?" he asks, still holding me tight.

"You walked into the building as if you were looking for something… you got to the fourth floor when someone hit you from the right with a two by four then again from behind. Then you were surrounded by a dozen or more people hitting and kicking you." I recalled starting to cry again.

"It's okay, I'm right here." he said soothingly.

"Someone came out of the shadows and it devastated you. I couldn't see the person's face clearly but it was definitely someone you know." I said panicky as I started to cry again.

"Shhh it's okay. It's okay." he said as he pulled my head into his chest.

Min-jah held me tightly until I finally stopped crying.

I double knotted the laces on my work shoes and stood up with a deep sigh.

"Are you sure you should go to work today?" Min-jah asks concerned.

"Yes," I sighed, "I can't just sit around after having a vision I need to distract myself or else I'll go crazy." I answered teary eyed.

"Okay okay." Min-jah says as he uses his sleeve to wipe my tears.

I waved goodbye as Min-jah dropped me off at the bus stop down the road. I took a deep breath as the bus pulled to a stop. Opening its doors I instantly stepped inside.

Min-jah, with the blinds drawn, sat in his office leaning forward at his desk with both his thumbs pressed against his bottom lip, his fingers intertwined together. He tapped his foot rapidly as he went over in his head what Joon had seen. Although already slightly suspecting his uncle to be behind the recent attempts on his life to get the company. He thought it would still be pretty devastating if his uncle really were the one behind it all. Not really wanting to suspect his uncle he certainly couldn't rule him out either. With a heavy sigh Min-jah reaches up and pushes the black button on his office phone.

"Seon, get me Byung-woo." he demands.

Byung-woo enters to find the office pitch black.

"Why's it so dark in here?" Byung-woo questions as he makes his way to the windows.

"I was thinking." Min-jah interjects coldly.

"About?" Byung-woo pries pulling the blinds open.

"Can you find out what my uncle has been up too outside the office?" Min-jah asks boldly.

"I'm sure I could." Byung-woo answers nonchalantly while still opening windows.

"I want to know about anything that seems even the slightest bit suspicious." Min-jah states.

"When do you want it?" Byung-woo says catching onto the seriousness of Min-jah's request.

"Today." Min-jah answers.

I put my headphones in as I poured a giant bowl of melted chocolate into a large 20cm thick rectangular mold using a bar to smooth out the bubbles. Moving all ten molds into the coolers, I started melting the white chocolate. With the white chocolate melted, I poured a line down the side of a flexible rubber flower petal molds. Using a small icing spatula to spread the chocolate I flipped over the molds to drain out the excess chocolate. I stared in silence as I waited for the flower petals to harden. Once ready I carefully took them out one by one.

Using an airbrush I painted the tips of the petals a light pink color. Placing a tiny drop of white chocolate on parchment paper I carefully began to assemble the flower. Placing five petals around the small dot I filled the center with milk chocolate and moved on to the next. Two more batches of petals were made and were colored a light orange followed by a light blue.

With the counters filled with tiny white flowers with colored tips the chocolate rectangle molds were ready. Using stencils Fei, Deok-su, and I cut out various shapes out of the chocolate molds. Making more chocolate rectangles as needed until we finally had all the pieces needed. Using more melted milk chocolate we began to piece together the shapes until we assembled a large milk chocolate structure the shape of the Eiffel Tower. Using a food safe spray gun Fei, while on a ladder, started at the top of the structure and painted it a darker rustic color to match the real thing. Deok-su and I began making chocolate vines with leaves using molding chocolate and painting them a forest green color.

Once the structure and vines were dry Fei and Deok-su began wrapping the vines crawling all the way up the structure. I followed closely behind them placing the colored chocolate flowers in various designs scattered up the climbing vines. Standing at the top of the ladder I reach to place the final flower on the tip top when the ladder shakes making me stumble. My heart stops as I quickly grab the top and Deok-su grabs the bottom of the ladder With a weary chuckle I let out a nervous breath as I steady my heart.

I slowly reach out and firmly place the last flower on the vine that wraps around the very top of the structure. I let out a sigh with a smile as everyone cheers as the order is complete.

I slowly climb down the ladder and take off the latex gloves. Going around giving everyone high-fives to celebrate, Fei stopped short when he reached me. Clenching my hands in a fist tightly I took a deep breath and relaxed my hand. Smiling I quickly gave him a high five instead. The celebration instantly stopped as Fei stood there with his hand up in complete shock. I tossed the gloves on the counter as I walked past him.

"I can go home now right Mr. Wei?" I asked over the deafening silence in the kitchen.

Shocked as well, Mr. Wei could only nod his head in agreement.

"Alright I'll see you guys tomorrow. Good work today." I say with a salute as I walk out the kitchen.

Still standing in shock Fei slowly lowered his hand.

"D-d-did he just touch my hand?" Fei finally stutters out.

Walking with Yuki-ji I laughed out loud as I remembered the look on all their faces.

"So it's getting better?" Yuki-ji asks with a smile.

"Ah yeah. I'm learning to control it." I say touching the crystal through my clothes.

"That's great." she says with a smile.

"Yeah." I agreed.

"What made you want to get help?" she asked puzzled.

"I uh met someone who made it easy." I answered quietly.

"Oooh" she mocked, "Who's the lucky lady?" she asks playfully as she elbows me.

"Well a guy actually." I said sheepishly.

"Oh." she said flatly.

"Yeah…" I said nervously.

After a few minutes of awkward silence she finally spoke.

"Does he make you happy?" she interrogates.

"Incredibly." I answered unhesitant.

She stared at me intensely as we rounded the corner to her house.

"That makes me happy." she finally says with a sigh.

"Ha I'll have to introduce you two someday." I say with a smile.

"Yeah someday." she repeats with a smile.

I waved goodbye to her and she rushed up her stairs and into her house. I smiled as I turned around to go meet Min-jah.

My phone rings and without looking I immediately answered after one ring.

"I'm-"

"That was fast, were you waiting for my call?" an unfamiliar male voice interrupts.

Frozen in place I stopped walking and stared straight ahead into the darkness in front of me.

"I don't understand why you walk her home every night. It's kind of annoying actually." his voice hisses with irritation.

Remaining silent I shifted the weight to the heels of my feet to spin around slowly looking at my surroundings.

"Aw-wa how am I supposed to find you in the dark if you don't make any noise?" his voice whines through the phone.

I start to breath heavily through my mouth as I frantically look around me seeing nothing but darkness.

"There we go, I can just follow the sound of your breathing." his voice laughs in my ear.

I instantly cover my mouth with my hand to quiet my breathing.

"Ready or not... here I come..." his voice suddenly echoed around me.

Flinching I instantly took off running as fast I could as the sound of his voice laughing hysterically came from the phone and from behind me. The bus stop comes into view and I start running faster as I see Min-jah patiently waiting for me by the car. Surprised Min-jah quickly catches me as I fling myself into his arms. Trembling, I manage to give Min-jah my phone. He looks at the caller identification before quickly putting the phone to his ear.

"Hello?" Min-jah quickly asks.

"Aww-aw he made it back to base... shoot maybe next time." the voice mocks.

"I thought I warned you to stay away from him." Min-jah hisses while looking around.

"Don't worry, our game will start soon." the voice laughs before hanging up the phone.

Holding me tightly Min-jah frantically searches through all the people around us before ushering me into the car. He slams my door closed and quickly runs around to the other side. Once inside the car he grabs my face to make me look at him.

"Are you okay? Are you hurt?" he asks frantically.

"I-I-I'm okay." I manage to stutter out.

He lets out a sigh as he pulls me over the center console into a hug.

"Let's go home, yeah?" he asks, more calmly.

"Mmm." I answered quietly.

CHAPTER 11

Min-jah strokes Joon's hair gently as he was finally able to get him to fall asleep. He glances at Joon's face to see his eyes were red and puffy from crying. Still sniffling, Joon hugs Mr. Snuggles tighter. Startled as his phone started ringing Min-jah quickly answered it.

"Hello?" he whispers.

"I have the information you wanted." Byung-woo says.

Glancing over at Joon Min-jah quietly leaves the room.

"Bring it over." Min-jah demands closing the door behind him.

Byung-woo with files in hand opens the door to find Min-jah sitting in the living room already waiting.

"What has he been up to?" Min-jah asks before Byung-woo could even enter the room.

"Besides his usual gambling habit he has been visiting an abandoned construction site quite frequently over the years." Byung-woo states handing Min-jah some paperwork.

Min-jah flips through the papers stopping as he comes across the name of the construction site, K mall apartments.

"What has he been doing here?" Min-jah asks looking up at Byung-woo.

"That I don't know, he drives himself there doesn't take anyone from his security team with him. He brought his secretary Ki-ha with him once but that was a few months ago." Byung-woo explains.

"How often does he go?" Min-jah asks.

"It varies sometimes once a month, others as many as three times a month." Byung-woo lays out.

Min-jah stares down at an aerial shot of his uncle looking back as he gets out of his car.

"Something is strange though, since your inauguration he has visited this site twelve times in the past two months." Byung-woo points out.

Min-jah turns his head sharply up towards Byung-woo in shock.

"I need to go see what he is up to." Min-jah jumps up.

"Whoa, whoa it's the middle of the night and what are you going to do anyways?" Byung-woo argues as he grabs Min-jah.

"It doesn't matter, I need to go right now." Min-jah urges.

"Stop, stop." Byung-woo pushes, "Let's do this I'll put together a small group of people that I trust and we go together?" Byung-woo purposes.

"No, I want you to stay here and protect Joon. I'll go alone." Min-jah counters.

"Protect Joon?" Byung-woo questions.

"Yes, I can't bet on the chance that my uncle doesn't know about him, especially after all the rumors spreading at the office." Min-jah says, glancing at him. "If something were to happen to him I couldn't live with myself. You are the only person I can trust with him." he pleads.

Byung-woo looks at the desperation in Min-jah's expression before he lets out a heavy sigh followed by a smile.

"Alright I'll stay here and protect him." Byung-woo agreed.

Byung-woo walks out of the house quickly glancing back as he pulls out his phone.

"Put together two teams of your most trustworthy men." Byung-woo says quickly and then hangs up the phone.

He tosses the phone into the passenger seat as he quickly drives away.

Sitting down in a brown recliner wearing a black robe and matching slippers flipping through the newspaper, Hong-gi looks up to Ki-ha entering the room.

"He's going to the construction site." Ki-ha says with a bow.

"Excellent." Hong-gi says while he flips a page of the paper.

Standing with a worried expression on my face as Min-jah proceeds to put on his shoes in front of the door.

"I promise I will be fine. I just talked to Byung-woo and he is already on his way over with a few guys to help protect you just in case. I'll only be gone a few hours and then I'll come right back." Min-jah reassures me.

He grabs my arms and shrinks down so he can look into my eyes.

"I promise." he says as he kisses my forehead.

I sigh unconvinced as he waves goodbye and closes the door. I turned around hesitantly and headed back upstairs to the bedroom. Min-jah pulled into the dirt driveway followed by a large black van. Min-jah stares up into the empty partially made building as several men in black suits walk up behind him.

"Alright let's go." Min-jah demands as he walks toward the building.

While walking up the stairs to the fourth floor Min-jah gets a suspiciously weird feeling. Carefully he pushes open the door to the fourth floor and walks in slowly. He looks around to see large pieces of hanging plastic and an empty floor that was littered with small pieces of trash. Out of nowhere as Joon had seen a two by four is suddenly flung at him from the right. Swiftly dodging by ducking the piece of wood hits the door to the floor slamming it shut. He then remembers the second hit from behind and rolls away as another piece shatters as it hits the floor. Quickly standing up Min-jah found himself surrounded by men welding large pieces of wood and metal bats.

With his fists up the circle of men chuckle as they close around him swinging around their weapons. Trying to keep his eyes on all the men one man with a bat suddenly launches at him swinging. Min-jah spins to his left making the man just barely miss his shot. He instantly punches the man in the back of the head so hard the man slips on the dirt and knocks himself out by hitting his head on the floor.

Another man with a piece of wood screams out as he runs toward Min-jah. He grabs the man's hand and swiftly wraps his right leg around the neck of the man and flips him to the floor. Still having a hold of the man's hand Min-jah violent twists right breaking it almost instantly. The whole circle of men then started to attack blindly. While avoiding most of the hits one managed to land a clean hit to his stomach with a two by four. Min-jah gasping for breath quickly jumps through the hanging plastic followed by three men.

Min-jah hides behind one of the pieces and waits for one to walk through. As soon as he sees him Min-jah upper cuts him in the jaw instantly knocking him out. He quickly moves by jumping over the half wall to have a bat instantly swung at him. Barely managing to dodge the bat Min-jah looks up at the man in shock.

He quickly grabs the bat with one hand and using the other to lift him up Min-jah runs his feet up the length of the man's body kicking him in the face. Landing on his feet with the bat still in his hand Min-jah looks at the remaining five men. Panting heavily the men start closing in on him. Min-jah flips the bat around so he is holding the handle he smacks the piece of wood one swung at him using his elbow to hit the guy in the face. He quickly ducks as another piece comes flying at him making it hit the third guy instead.

Min-jah swings the bat at the ankles of another, tripping him. He starts walking backwards while the last three start walking towards him. Suddenly he is hit from behind Min-jah hollers out as a metal bat smashes his left knee. Using the bat in his hand Min-jah catches himself before he completely collapses on the floor. Another man from behind kicks the bat out of Min-jah's hand, making him fall.

With a swift kick to his stomach Min-jah is left gasping for breath. He struggles to crawl away when he is kicked in the stomach again. Struggling to breath Min-jah rolls on his back holding his stomach. Pulled up by his hair one of the men dropped kicked him in the face. With his ears ringing Min-jah rolls over coughing and spitting out blood. One man ties his hands together while another two force him up on his feet.

Unable to stand on his own, the two men who forced him up hold him by his arms. Min-jah struggles to hold his head up as he breathes heavily occasionally spitting out blood that was dripping from his nose. The ringing in his ears begins to subside while he tightly closes his eyes and winces from the pain. When an all too familiar laugh starts coming towards him from the back of the room Min-jah's eyes spring open. Joon's words about who the culprit was began to echo in his ears as he slowly raised his head.

"Wow I must say you are a lot tougher than I gave you credit for." Laughed a familiar voice from behind the hanging plastic.

Laying in bed reading a book I hear the doorbell suddenly start to ring, perplexed I closed the book and headed down stairs. I quickly rushed down the stairs as the doorbell rang out again.

"Byung-woo don't you... have... a... key?" I trailed off slowly as I opened the door and four large strange men were staring at me.

Without warning one reached inside and placed his large hands on my shoulders and forcibly yanked me out the door with a quick gasp.

"B-Byung-woo?!" Min-jah stuttered out in a breathless whisper.

Byung-woo walks out of the plastic, turning up his nose as he steps over one of the men who was left knocked unconscious on the floor.

I came too lying on the ground with a bag over my head and my wrists and ankles bound tightly together. I quickly pull the bag off my head and immediately have to cover my eyes from the direct ray of sunlight that's shining into the space I was being held. I place my hand down on the ground next to me and realize I was sitting in a layer of water. I looked around and realized that I was sitting in an underground tunnel aside from the ray of light. Everything else around me was pitch black. I began to struggle with the ropes holding me violently splashing around in the water.

"Hey be quiet!" hollers an unfamiliar voice.

Flinching I realized unlike in my dream I wasn't alone I followed his orders and stopped splashing.

Staring as his eyes filled with tears Min-jah couldn't believe what he was seeing. Rubbing his eyes roughly Min-jah blinked rapidly as Byung-woo made his way around the unconscious men on the ground. Byung-woo knelt down in front of him chuckling as a tear rolled down Min-jah's dirt covered face.

"W-why?" Min-jah whispered defeatedly.

"Why?" Byung-woo repeated with a laugh. "Let me tell you a little secret. Well it's not really a *little* secret it's actually a pretty fucking big one." he chuckled.

Following him with his eyes Min-jah stared as Byung-woo paced in a circle.

"You see before you were born there was a little boy who was suddenly born from a housemaid of a very wealthy family. Now how did she get pregnant? Well as most of the rumors say it was the butler but seeing as he disappeared the night before their forced marriage, I'm willing to bet he wasn't the father. Dangerously vicious rumors began to spread as she refused to give up the name of the father. Only on her deathbed, after keeping it a secret for so many years, she finally let the name of the father slip through her lips." Byung-woo goes on staring coldly at Min-jah. "Do you know what she said?"

Min-jah stared in silence as Byung-woo kneels in front of him again. Staring at his face Byung-woo grew impatient as Min-jah didn't answer. Irritated, he stands back up with a huff as he chuckled in disbelief.

"You can't be serious? I know you aren't too quick to catch things but I spelled it out for you! Lan Kim-su! She said your father's name!" Byung-woo shouts out in anger.

"W-what?" Min-jah stutters.

"Ah there it is!" Byung-woo hollers throwing up his hands. "Imagine my shock, at seventeen when I found out that the boy I called my best friend was actually my younger brother and the man he called father was also mine."

Unable to say anything Min-jah stared in disbelief as Byung-woo angrily continued to talk.

"You know... after that I began to wonder, did he know? Of course it wasn't until shortly after my mother's sudden death, when he started treating me coldly, that I knew. After that I tried everything to be the closest person to you so he couldn't find an excuse to get rid of me like he did with my mother. It was later, much later I learned of the truth behind my mother's death. Your mother somehow found out the truth about me and out of anger, or maybe just pure jealousy, she had my mother killed. That was when I decided that I was going to take everything. Everything that was supposed to be mine." he chuckles, "Getting rid of her was actually pretty easy. I mean who eats something just because a child gave it to her?" Byung-woo laughs.

Filled with anger Min-jah begins to struggle against the men holding him.

"I was truly very disappointed when father dearest killed over from cancer honestly. I wanted to see the look on his face as I killed everyone he loved and took everything he worked so hard for. With him out of the way though I realized I had one major problem." Byung-woo says as he kneels in front of the struggling Min-jah.

"You're insane." Min-jah growls continuing to struggle.

"Maybe, but who's fault is that?" he sighs while standing up. "You are seriously hard to kill though. I tried a bunch of different things throughout the years but you either ended up with broken bones or minor injuries. After father's death I got a little too excited being so close to my goal, I even tried to assassinate you." he laughs. "Shockingly you even managed to escape that with only a scratch. So I went for a more discreet route but you surprisingly caught on much quicker than I expected. It wasn't until *you* told me it was all because of that pâtissier Joon of course." Byung-woo stops.

"Joon?" Min-jah whispers as his eyes widen. "What have you done to him!" he shouts angrily.

"Relax, as long as he behaves and I get what I want, I won't hurt him." Byung-woo says as a man hands him a large crowbar. "So if you could just quietly die right here. Once I take over the company I'll take care of your precious Joon for the *rest of his life*, I promise." he says with a wicked smile as he raises the crowbar above his head.

Startled as a sudden loud shout comes from behind them, Min-jah sees a dozen or so men rushing in wearing police uniforms with their weapons drawn run up behind Byung-woo. The two men holding Min-jah drop him frantically looking around as the police surround them. With his eyes closed Min-jah sighs with relief as he sits up on his knees. Byung-woo, still holding up the crowbar chuckles with irritation as the police continue to shout orders.

Quickly glaring over at Min-jah he clenches his fists tightly as he stepped forward to swing the crowbar. Glancing over Min-jah sees Byung-woo coming at him and instinctively he shields his head with his hands. Opening his eyes slowly as the expected hit doesn't come he looks up to see Detective Ma standing in front of him.

"Whoa there." he growls in his gravelly voice.

Byung-woo chuckles again staring at the detective who had his weapon drawn and aimed right at him.

"Give me a reason." he growls coldly.

Smiling Byung-woo tosses the crowbar as he kneels on the ground putting his hands on his head. Staring coldly at Min-jah as another officer puts cuffs on him he suddenly cracks a grin while being dragged away. Detective Ma holsters his gun irritated as he turns toward Min-jah.

"Are you okay?" he asks untying Min-jah's hands.

"I'll live." Min-jah answers.

Detective Ma chuckles as he helps Min-jah to his feet. Sirens blaring and lights flashing there's a dozen or more police vehicles surrounding the building. Min-jah walks through the chaotic sea of people and cars as he catches a glimpse of Byung-woo being forced into the back of a police car. Byung-woo smiles wickedly as he stares at Min-jah while the door is slammed closed.

"Can I talk to him?" Min-jah asks while still staring.

"Yeah." Detective Ma answers while following his gaze.

Min-jah walks up to the side of the vehicle nodding to the police officer inside who rolls down the back window slightly.

"If you had told me I would have willingly given you everything." Min-jah says.

"Ha. Is that really what you would have done?" Byung-woo scoffs.

"Yes." Min-jah answers with no hesitation. "Because I always thought of you as my older brother anyway I would have happily handed everything to you." he explains.

Byung-woo looks up in shock when he starts to chuckle.

"Is this really what you want to talk about?" he scoffs.

"What?" Min-jah asks confused.

"Ha you truly are a dense motherfucker. I'm sure word has already spread what has happened here. Now just what do you think will happen to *him* anyway?" Byung-woo says with a cackling laugh.

Stumbling backwards as the police car drives away Min-jah starts to hyperventilate as Detective Ma catches him.

"What? What is it?" Detective Ma asks while holding him up.

"Joonie-ah." Min-jah softly whispers.

Sitting in the back of an ambulance Min-jah slowly breathes using a can of oxygen while holding the crystal necklace in his hand when he glances upward. A dark mid-sized vehicle pulls in joining the sea of cars. The driver rushes to the other side of the car swiftly opening the door. Hong-gi gets out while looking around followed by his secretary Ki-ha. Noticing Min-jah squinting at them from the ambulance they made their way quickly through the crowd.

"Detective Ma." Hong-gi greets while shaking his hand.

"Director Lan." Detective Ma bows.

Shocked Min-jah stares as they exchange greetings clearly having already met each other.

"U-uncle?" Min-jah finally says.

"I'm sorry it had to go this far but it was the only way to finally catch him." Hong-gi says.

"So you knew?" Min-jah says accusingly.

"Now let's not get angry already just hear him out." Detective Ma says apprehensively already sensing the growing tension.

"Ha." Min-jah scoffs.

Looking down guiltily rubbing his hands together Hong-gi begins to explain.

"I didn't know until your father told me while he was in the hospital. He made me promise to protect you. It was his last wish. At first I didn't believe it but then as I observed him I began to see something suspicious. I conducted an investigation into all the accidents you had and anything that might seem suspicious when I learned the truth of your mother's death and that he was hurting you intentionally. I tried to gather the evidence so I could turn him in but everything was circumstantial nothing would stick. Even with the assassination attempt he kept a large enough distance so that nothing would lead back to him." Hong-gi lays out.

"Why didn't you tell me?" Min-jah asks.

"I didn't want him to do something rash if he knew I was on to him. So I made myself look suspicious hoping he would try to use me as a scapegoat for when he did make his move." Hong-gi says. "So a couple times a month I would meet here with Detective Ma to keep him informed of everything. I just wanted to protect you."

Min-jah glares at him angrily for several minutes before he lets out a sigh.

"I'll forgive you if you help me with one thing." Min-jah purposes.

"Whatever you need." Hong-gi agrees.

"Byung-woo kidnapped someone who is highly important to me and I need to find him quickly." Min-jah explains.

"I think I can help with that." comes a small voice behind Hong-gi.

Hong-gi turns around allowing Min-jah to see where the voice had come from.

"Then do it." Min-jah commands.

"Yes Sir." Ki-ha bows before swiftly walking away.

"Oh, there's one more thing I need your help with." Min-jah says quickly before Hong-gi walks away.

Hong-gi turns to look at Min-jah as he climbs down out of the ambulance.

CHAPTER 12

Sitting quietly up against the wall pressing my fingertips together trying to think of a plan to escape. I noticed something sharp sticking out of the water in front of me. I inched myself closer slowly so as to not make too much noise with the water. Once I could easily reach it, I quickly picked it up and scooted back against the wall. Causing a little too much noise as the guard glared at me from the opening of the tunnel. I flashed a smile and a quick peace sign with my empty hand as I leaned back against the wall until he looked away.

I opened my hand slowly to see that I grabbed a pointed black rock that looked like it might be sharp enough to cut the rope. I began to make quick work sawing at the rope around my ankles quietly. Arms aching I had made it about half way when suddenly a phone started to ring. He glanced at me before he stood up and walked away to answer the phone. Watching him until even his shadow disappeared I started sawing at the rope even faster.

I heard his footsteps splashing in the water as he returned. Panicking, I started to pull my ankles apart as I continued to rub the rock against the rope. His shadow glided across the wall catching my attention with a tiny bit left to cut. I quickly hid the rock in my hands as he walked into the tunnel with me.

"Bad news for you little one." he says with a bat in his hand.

Quickly flashing a glance at the bat and then back to his face dropping the rock I use my hands to push myself away from him.

"W-what's that?" I said, gulping nervously as he walked closer.

"Well the Big Boss didn't get what he wanted." he explained dropping the top of the bat in the water dragging it as he walked.

"B-Big boss? I repeated scooting away even farther.

"That's right, so I've been instructed to tie up loose ends." he said as he slowly pulled the bat up above him.

I stared wide eyed as the bat slowly raised in the air and let out a loud gasp the bat came swinging down.

Standing in the police station Min-jah anxiously paced back and forth in front of Detective Ma's desk. Irritated by watching him Detective Ma groans as he stands up.

"Look, can you please just…" Detective Ma growls as he forces Min-jah to sit in a chair.

"Sorry…" Min-jah apologizes as he starts to rapidly tap his foot.

Sighing and rolling his eyes Detective Ma shakes his head as he goes to sit down. Glancing at him nervously tapping his foot and looking at the entrance of the police station Detective Ma leans forward.

"Who is Joon to you to have you in this state?" he asks interrogatively.

Min-jah stops tapping his foot as he turns his attention to Detective Ma who was staring at him.

"He's the single most important person in my life." Min-jah answers coldly.

"But do you even know him? You guys only met a few months ago." Detective Ma inquires.

"I know he is the cutest-"

"Cute?" Detective Ma repeats.

"Sweetest, most selfless person that has ever existed. Who tries his hardest to make sure those around him are happy and never feel lonely when it's really him who's the loneliest. He's someone who doesn't smile often but when he does it can light up the entire room. He saves strangers without hesitation even when it could mean to put himself in harm's way. And even if he does end up hurt he will do it again. He's someone who doesn't realize just how important he is and I need to protect him because no one else will otherwise. Especially cynical people like you." Min-jah says, raising his voice louder and louder until the entire police station was listening.

Min-jah sat staring at the detective fuming with anger when a voice suddenly interrupted.

"Sir, I found him." Ki-ha says breaking the silence.

I gasped as I looked over to see the bat engraved into the wall panting as I looked up. Chuckling he instantly pulls the bat out of the wall.

"You are quick." he laughs as he swings the bat again.

Quickly rolling away the last bit of remaining rope around my ankles snaps. Realizing I scramble to my feet as the bat splashes the water next to me. I dash down the dark tunnel blindly.

"Where are you running too?" he laughs as he walks to follow.

Panting heavily I run my hand along the wall of the tunnel to find my way. The wall suddenly dropped off panting I stopped to look back. With a loud echoing bang coming from the direction I ran from I rushed down the turn with no hesitation. Lighting his way with a flashlight the man stops at the fork in the tunnels and quietly listens. The sound of water splashing violently catches his attention as he shines the light down the dark tunnel. With a smirk he makes his way down the tunnel playfully swinging the bat in his hand.

Detective Ma and Min-jah quickly rush outside followed by a dozen other officers who swiftly get into their vehicles.

"Here get in." Detective Ma demands unlocking a beat up old clunker.

"You can't be serious?" Min-jah says breathlessly as he watches Detective Ma climb into the vehicle.

Sirens blaring and lights flashing a small fleet of police vehicles led by the Detective's clunker sped down the main road. Blowing through red light after red light Min-jah squeezes the handle attached to the roof of the Detective's car. Honking his horn and shouting as the cars in front are too slow to move Detective Ma growls angrily. Quickly glancing over at Min-jah Detective Ma begins to honk his horn again and speeds up.

Running I glanced behind me to see a streak of light bouncing around in the dark as he chased me. I followed the wall finding another turn frantic I quickly turned as the light got closer. I took turn after turn until I lost all sense of where I was or where I had come from. Hearing water splashing behind me and seeing the shine of the light in the water I started running again. While running I passed the opening of a tunnel that had light at the end of it. I instantly stopped and stared at it as if in a trance. The sound of water splashing behind me breaks me loose as I quickly move into the tunnel.

The fleet of police vehicles come to a screeching stop in the parking lot of an abandoned water treatment plant. Officers instantly jumped out and began to search the area quickly. Min-jah climbs out of the Detective's car looking around as officers rush into the main building while others begin to search the outside.

Halfway down the tunnel I stopped running as I began to hear police sirens in the distance getting closer. I let out a nervous laugh as I started running down the tunnel again. Reaching the end of the tunnel I shielded my eyes from the sunlight from the opening to the surface.

"Min-jah!" I shouted as loud as I could.

The large man stops walking as a voice echoes through the tunnels leading the way. With a smirk he turns toward the sound.

Leaning against the vehicle Min-jah anxiously waits for news as Detective Ma comes out of the main building shaking his head.

"He's not inside." Detective Ma says disheartedly.

Disappointed Min-jah crouches holding his head as he lets out a frustrated groan. Min-jah stands up and roughly rubs his mouth while he looks around again.

"Look, this is a large place we will keep looking." Detective Ma says trying to sooth him.

A sudden small voice in the distance catches Min-jah's attention.

"I promise we wil-" Detective Ma continues.

"Wait." Min-jah interrupts.

"What is-" he tries to ask.

"Shhhh." Min-jah shushes him.

His eyes widen as the voice reaches him again.

"Joonie-ah." Min-jah whispers before taking off running.

Detective Ma whistles loudly and waves over some more officers before he quickly follows behind him.

"Joon!" Min-jah shouts again desperately as he sprints down the dirt road.

"Min-jah!" I shouted again a little discouraged wondering if he could even hear me.

Glancing behind me quickly to see if he had found me yet. I step out of the tunnel into the open area to get closer to the opening to try again when I hear a voice shouting my name.

"Min-jah!" I shouted back surprised.

He slides into the opening knocking dirt into the hole almost falling in himself. I covered my eyes from the dirt coughing as I looked up to see Min-jah looking down at me with a large smile. Running past the beginning of the tunnel the man quickly stopped as he looked down and saw me standing at the end. Hearing the sirens he clenched his teeth as he quickly ran down the tunnel.

"Joonie-ah!" Min-jah says with a huge sigh of relief

"Min Min." I say back with tears in my eyes as I look up at him.

Relieved I smiled, letting out a sigh of relief, and closed my eyes. I opened them to see Min-jah's smile fade as he looked behind me. I turned around to meet the man swinging the bat hitting me in the head.

My ears started to ring loudly as my body crumbled underneath me. I hit my knees as the sound of my breathing drowns out Min-jah's voice shouting my name. My head hits the ground with a splash as the man quickly dashes back down the tunnel. Min-jah instantly jumps down into the tunnel followed by two officers who immediately ensue in a foot chase.

Min-jah quickly scoops up my head to get it out of the water. Tapping my cheeks rapidly Min-jah looked panicked as he noticed the blood mixed with water flow down the side of my face.

"Hey, hey." Min-jah says rapidly tapping my cheeks.

Quickly checking the rest of my body for injuries Min-jah gently brushes the hair off my face.

"Joon. Joon I'm right here. Can you hear me? Joonie-ah?" Min-jah pleads in a choked voice.

Unable to speak, I stared at his face feeling relieved that I got to see him again. I slowly blinked as the echoing sound of Min-jah's voice calling my name soothed me. As I felt myself losing consciousness I reached my still bounded hands up and wiped a tear from his cheek gently with my finger.

"Joon?" he asked, surprised grabbing my hand.

"I-I'm fine" I managed to breathlessly stutter out as my eyes rolled into the back of my head.

"Joonie-ah?! Joon?!" Min-jah shouts in a sobbing panic.

Detective Ma jumps down into the hole to see Min-jah sobbing loudly holding Joon tightly rocking back and forth. A police officer tapped on Min-jah's shoulder, brushing off the officer he continued to hold him. The officer pulled on Min-jah's arm to get him to release Joon, pulling his arm out of the officer's grip he shoved the officer away as he cradled Joon's head. Nodding toward three other police officers they forcibly removed Min-jah from Joon's side. As if everything was moving in slow motion Min-jah watched as Joon's head fell back into the water. Screaming and fighting with all his might the four police officers struggled to hold him back while the paramedics rushed to Joon's aid. Sighing in defeat, Detective Ma painfully looks away as Min-jah continues to scream while being dragged away.

A light rhythmic beeping sound woke me up. I slowly opened my eyes as a wave of pain flooded over me. Groaning painfully I sat up and took off the air tube that was on my face. Instantly getting hit with a splitting headache on top of the pain in my body I reached up and grabbed my head feeling the gauze that was wrapped around it. Glancing at my hand that had an IV drip and a small grey clamp on my index finger with a cord that led to the machine that was the source of the beeping.

I looked around the room to see a bouquet of flowers with a 'get well soon' balloon tied to an empty vase sitting on the table. Reaching up I rubbed my neck finding the crystal necklace was gone. Panicked, I quickly searched all around me finding it hanging from the side rail of the hospital bed. I carefully untied it and held the clear crystal in my hand when the door to the room suddenly slid open. Standing in the doorway holding a pitcher of water and fresh flowers was Yuki-ji. Dropping the flowers and the pitcher splashing water everywhere she quickly turns and runs back down the hall.

"He's awake!" she shouts running down the hall.

One MRI scan and a rather long physical checkup later, I learned I had been in a coma for three months. With no signs of ever being able to wake up, the doctors could only call it a miracle. Yuki-ji then tells me everything that happened from a handsome stranger paying for everything to what happened with the people who were involved with my kidnapping.

Overwhelmed I sat in silence on the hospital bed holding the crystal necklace in my hand staring out the window.

"Joon?" Yuki-ji says as she walks into the room.

"Mmm." I say with a smile hiding the necklace.

"I'm so glad you finally woke up!" she says hoarsely trying not to cry.

"I'm sorry I made you worry..." I say quietly as she sits next to me.

"Oh my gosh I was crazy worried but not even close compared to the handsome guy that comes every single day." she says quickly, releasing her breath.

I stared at her as she shook her head in disbelief.

"I don't know who he is to you but besides paying for everything I can tell he cares deeply for you. Cute too, tall, always wearing a suit, oh and he's surrounded by security guards." she explains.

I look down and smile as she continues to ramble on describing Min-jah.

"Who is he anyways?" she asks looking at me.

I grabbed her hand softly, I saw a peaceful scene of a much older version of Yuki-ji laying in a quiet hospital room as a gentle smile faded away peacefully passing away. I glanced up at her with a smile happy the vision had changed.

"He's my boyfriend." I answer.

Min-jah sighed heavily as he placed a piece of paper down on his desk. Standing up he walked over to the window while looking at the clear crystal around his neck. He leaned against the back of the leather couch as a tear escaped and rolled down his cheek. Quickly covering his eyes he pressed down firmly and took several deep breaths to stop the urge to cry again. A soft knock came from the door startling him. He quickly sniffles and wipes his face as he turns around.

"Come in." he croaks.

The door creaks open as Ki-ha walks in holding a stack of documents in his arms.

"It's time for the board meeting Sir." Ki-ha says with a bow.

"Right, lead the way." he sniffles, grabbing his coat.

Min-jah sat at the head of a large table that had a dozen old men lining the sides.

"You see the fact that you are gay and that your lover is in a coma became public, our stocks have been on the decline. Which is worrisome for some of our shareholders." one overweight grey haired man said using a laser to point at a graph.

"Some people are actually heavily boycotting our products and places of businesses." said another.

Scattered muttering erupted between the group as Min-jah silently watched. Ki-ha looks at Min-jah and widens his eyes to urge him to say something. Min-jah shook his head in disagreement as the men continued to bicker amongst themselves. Hong-gi sighed as he crossed his arms and leaned back in his chair. The volume of the conversations began to rise before Min-jah slammed his hand on the table loudly stopping all chatter.

"Since the matter of who I am in love with is so important to you all let me shed some light on the matter. Since it went public over the course of three months our stocks have only dropped by three percent. Now I don't know about you guys but if you can't find a solution to counteract that measly three percent. Why are you guys even directors for this company?" Min-jah lays out harshly.

The gentlemen all quietly shift in their seats awkwardly as Min-jah gets up and starts walking around the table.

"As for these protests and boycotts as long as they don't turn violent and harm any of the employees at the locations just let them be the people will vent out their anger and then get over it." Min-jah continues. "So focus on fixing the three percent or be prepared to find a new job gentleman." he warns as he walks out of the room.

Hong-gi begins to chuckle softly steadily growing to a loud laughter as the rest of the men around the table sit in silence. Irritated Min-jah opened the door to his office angrily leaving it open as Ki-ha followed him in. He tosses his coat over the large leather couch as he flops down on the other one with an exhausted sigh. Min-jah pulls out the crystal and rolls it in between his fingers.

"Has there been any change?" Min-jah asks flatly.

"No Sir there has been no reported change." Ki-ha answers sadly.

Min-jah leans forward with his elbows on his knees running his hands through his hair. He watches intently as the crystal swings back and forth in between his legs. The crystal's swinging begins to slow as a deep blue hue suddenly starts to fill the center. Min-jah quickly grabs the crystal as the color changes to a deep green.

"Hospital. Now." Min-jah demands.

Min-jah jumped out of the car before the driver could even come to a complete stop. He runs to the closest elevator hitting the up arrow rapidly impatiently he dashes to the stairs as the elevator doors open. Slamming the door open he looks up at the seemingly endless stairwell breathlessly. He quickly bounds up the stairs skipping three steps at a time. He burst through the door opening to the sixth floor panting pushing past people to get to the room. Standing in front of the door Min-jah breaths heavily in an attempt to stop panting. Shakily he reaches out his hand to grab the handle slowly opening the door.

Sitting in a wheelchair across the room looking out the window I slowly turned around as the door opened. My eyes immediately filled with tears as I looked at Min-jah standing in front of my door panting. I slowly stood up and turned nervously to face him.

"You got here fast." I said with a wry chuckle pointing at the crystal around my neck.

Min-jah instantly springs across the room and wraps his arms around me tightly. I quickly blinked as tears began to roll down my face hugging him back. He pulls me out of the hug and starts laughing as he grabs my face wiping my tears away with his thumbs. I laugh as I wipe his away too.

Laying on the bed Min-jah holds me tightly stroking the back of my head. I squeezed his hand tightly as I nestled my head on his chest.

"Oh!" Min-jah suddenly says. "I have something for you."

He quickly gets out of bed and swiftly walks to his coat where he rummages through the pockets before pulling out a small green square box. He turns around with a smile and crawls back onto the bed.

"Here." he says as he hands me the gift box.

Intrigued I opened the box to find a silver bracelet that had a single charm of a brown teddy bear wearing a sweater and at the end there was a flat heart shaped charm with the name "Joonie-ah♥" engraved into it. I quickly looked up at Min-jah who was shyly looking away from me.

"I-I had my uncle make them for me." he said softly.

"Them?" I questioned.

Min-jah pulled up his left sleeve to show he was wearing one with the matching white teddy bear and sweater with his heart saying "Min Min♥". I chuckled softly as he turned his face away to hide his red cheeks.

"Um there's also this." he said grabbing the bracelet out of the box.

He turned the heart sideways to show a tiny black switch.

"If you flip this switch a tracker will turn on and it will automatically send your location to my phone." he explains as he flips the switch and his phone immediately gets a notification.

"That way in case you are ever in any trouble and for whatever reason I'm not around I'll be able to find you." he says as he flips the switch off.

I smile at him as he puts the bracelet on my right wrist carefully. I instantly wrapped him in a hug tightly as soon as the bracelet was secured.

"I'm so happy to see you." I sigh.

"I'm happy to see you too." he says hugging me back.

I spent the next four days in the hospital taking a series of MRI's and CAT scans for my head and body. Surprised at how quickly my body was recovering the doctors finally agreed to discharge me. I walked out the front doors with a relieving sigh to see Min-jah waiting to take me home. I went by the bakery to see everyone, Mr. Wei immediately started ugly crying once I got there. He was ecstatic that I was finally out of the hospital but he wouldn't let me come back to work.

Sitting on the bed with Mr. Snuggles in my lap I was looking at the teddy bear bracelet.

"Look Mr. Snuggles a mini you." I said with a chuckle.

Min-jah then walks out of the bathroom with nothing but a towel wrapped around his waist using a smaller towel to dry his hair. I leaned back against my hands and lightly bit my bottom lip as I watched him walk across the room. Glancing up while drying his hair Min-jah caught a glimpse of me watching him continuing to dry his hair he smiles softly. Tossing the smaller towel aside Min-jah glances up at me as he crawls on the bed slowly making his way toward me.

Moving Mr. Snuggles out of my lap he lays his head in my lap. Looking down at him I shift the fringe of his bangs as he stares at me. Smiling, he reaches up and strokes my cheek.

"I think I love you Min Min." I say with a chuckle.

Smiling he sits up and pulls me by my chin and kisses me while we slowly lay down. Pressing his body against mine I tightly wrap my legs around his waist. He slowly starts kissing my neck as he slides his right hand under my shirt. I quickly try to stop him when he grabs both my hands and holds them above my head. He suddenly stops to look directly at me. Embarrassed under his intense gaze I looked away from him. He grabs my chin and softly pulls it making me look at him again.

"I think I love you too Joonie-ah." he answers softly.

His eyes darted quickly between my eyes and my lips kissing me again. His grip on my wrists tightened as he kissed me harder. As he pushed his body farther into my legs I wrapped them around him tighter. The towel wrapped around him came undone as he slid his hands up from my wrists to interlock his fingers tightly in between mine.

While laying in his arms I played with the fingers on his left hand while he gently stroked my hair while falling asleep. I slowly traced the edge of his hand with my fingertips as if I was trying to draw him. I snuggled deeper into the side of his body when my phone dings from the bedside table. I reached up and grabbed it nestling back into my spot as I unlocked my phone.

I sat up as my phone dings repeatedly showing different pictures of me from when I was a child to me now. As the pictures continued to flood in, the pictures shifted from far away surveillance type shots to more intimate and close up ones. Min-jah sits up and looks over my shoulder at all the pictures flooding my phone.

Don't you worry I'll find you...

I always do...

Shocked, I drop my phone and sink into Min-jah's warm comforting embrace. Staring coldly at the last message on the phone Min-jah squeezes me tighter as I tremble in fear.

CHAPTER 13

I sat quietly at the kitchen table as the sunlight slowly poured in from the large windows. Looking down at my hands in my lap Min-jah quietly came down the stairs. I glanced up at him as he walked past me sighing as he slipped into the chair across from me.

"What is it?" he asked concerned.

"I thought I had a good idea who was stalking me..." I said softly.

Min-jah's face instantly went hard and full of hate as the words came out of my mouth. I looked down biting my lip running my finger down the side of my now cold coffee.

"But this doesn't make any sense..." I sniffled and hugged myself tightly.

"Who?" Min-jah says sharply.

"I thought it was Yuki-ji's neighbor, since that's when the messages started... but..." I trailed off.

"But?" he urges.

"The pictures from last night... Some of them were from when I was thirteen still living at the orphanage. I didn't even know Yuki-ji let alone her neighbor." I explained.

Min-jah sat quietly staring right through me as if he was lost deep in thought. I sniffled loudly wiping my nose and my face as I sat curled up in the chair. Min-jah blinks rapidly as he turns his focus and glances over at me.

"For now I won't leave you alone," he says. "You will come with me to work."

"But…" I started.

"It will be fine." he interjected quickly. "I'm the Chairman who's going to argue with me?"

"…the bracelet." I said softly, shaking my wrist.

"That is for if you desperately need me and I'm not there. I don't want to give you the chance to actually use it." he argues.

Nodding my head in agreement knowing, by the look in his eyes, I wasn't going to be winning this argument. He pulled me up out of the chair with a sweet smile giving me a quick hug and a soft kiss on my forehead before we went upstairs to get ready.

I walked outside to find the driver already standing at the back with the car door opened and waiting.

"Let's go." Min-jah says walking out of the house.

Placing his hand around my waist squeezing tightly we made our way to the car. I sat quietly rubbing my hands together nervously as the car sped down the road. Glancing over Min-jah reached over placing his hand gently over mine with a sweet smile. That sweet smile of his and the gentle squeeze on my hands instantly melted my heart along with my nerves.

Pulling up to the building we were greeted by two rows of people that made a path that went all the way to the main doors. Dressed in solid black suits, black sunglasses, a small white cord attached to their right ear, and armed with a pistol on their hips they stood at attention. The car door opens and Min-jah immediately gets out. I slowly slid across to the opened door as I stared at the welcoming party.

Holding out his hand Min-jah smiles at me as I grab it and get out of the car. I looked down the aisle of people and saw a crowd coming towards us at a quick pace. At the front of the pack was an older gentleman, who was smiling widely, I immediately recognized as Min-jah's uncle. He approached us quickly grabbing my hand firmly with a large happy smile.

"I'm so glad to finally meet you." he says excitedly squeezing my hand.

I quickly glanced over at Min-jah who was covering his smile with his hand silently watching.

"Ah, I'm Lan Hong-gi, Min-jah's uncle." he explains happily.

"N-nice to finally meet you too." I chuckled nervously.

Still holding my hand Hong-gi's face lit up with even more happiness.

"Alright that's enough touching for you." Min-jah said playfully as he pulled my hand out of Hong-gi's grasp.

"Of course, of course." Hong-gi chuckles "Let's go inside."

Min-jah laughs softly as his uncle turns around walking swiftly back down the aisle towards the door. Turning towards me Min-jah gently shifted my hair on my forehead with a smile.

"Well it looks like he approves." he says with a smile as he grabs my hand tightly.

I grin shyly as Min-jah leads the way down the path of people to the main door. Entering the lobby Min-jah was greeted by employees nonchalantly and almost habitually followed by a stunned silence. The silence began to fill the lobby as they all stopped and stared as we made our way through. Apprehensive about everyone staring at me I squeezed Min-jah's hand tighter as we walked through the sea of eyes. Approaching the security gates Min-jah nodded toward the guard with a smile. Stunned the guard hit the button that opened all the gates staring as we walked through.

Standing by the elevator I could see the crowd of employees on the other side of the gates staring in awe. Light whispers began to travel through the crowd as we stood there. Min-jah lightly squeezed my hand as the doors to the elevator opened and we stepped inside. The doors opened up as a female employee holding a stack of papers in her hand was walking by. She glances over and lets out an audible gasp before quickly covering her mouth as we stepped out of the elevator.

"Seon, have you seen Ki-ha?" Min-jah asks.

Staring at me and then quickly looking down at our hands interlocked together and then back up at me she doesn't say a word.

"Seon?" Min-jah asks puzzled.

"Oh, he's uh waiting in your office already." she answers distractedly as she continues to stare at me.

"Thank you." Min-jah replies.

"Is there something on my face?" I whisper as he pulls me along behind him.

Left standing there Seon lets out a small whimper as some papers slowly slipped out of her hands.

Min-jah pushed open a pair of large doors leading to an office with furniture on one side and a large wooden desk on the other. Standing in the center of the room was a young man I've never seen before. Wearing a blue suit he quickly turned around as we entered the room.

"Good morning Chairman Lan, Park-Chul Joon." the man says with a bow.

"Good morning Ki-ha." Min-jah replies as he closes the office doors.

Min-jah motioned for me to take a seat on the large black leather couch as he made his way to the desk on the other side.

"Joon, this is Ki-ha. He is my new personal assistant. He will be in charge of making sure you are comfortable while you are inside this building." Min-jah explained as he sat down.

I glanced apprehensively over at the man standing as he gave me a small bow.

"What about you?" I ask quickly.

"I'm afraid I'll be too busy, but I'll be here in this room with you unless I have a board meeting." Min-jah answers with a sigh.

I sighed heavily as I glanced back over at Ki-ha.

"Forgive me for not being too friendly but the last personal assistant tried to have me killed." I say rudely glaring at Ki-ha.

"Joonie-ah." Min-jah says softly from across the room.

Ki-ha quickly held up his hand toward Min-jah with his head bowed.

"I understand Mr. Park-Chul." he says. "I'll do my best to earn your trust." Ki-ha said definitively as he bowed his head and swiftly left the room.

"What?" I huffed as I leaned back on the couch.

Min-jah shook his head and sighed as he grabbed the first binder on top of the stack on his desk.

Ki-ha lets out a discouraged sigh as he closes the office door.

"Psst."

"Psst."

Confused Ki-ha quickly looks around to find Seon hiding behind the divider on her desk. He instantly rolls his eyes as he walks over to her desk.

"Yes Seon?" Ki-ha asks annoyed.

"Who was that that came into the office holding Chairman Lan's hand?" she whispers cautiously.

"I swear you live off gossip don't you." Ki-ha says under his breath.

Appalled Seon swiftly came out of hiding.

"No I do not." she objected fiercely.

"Right. Then why does it matter who that young man is?" Ki-ha asks mockingly as he walks away.

"Then is it actually true? Is he really?" Seon shouts after him.

Ki-ha exaggeratedly throws his hands up and shrugs as he continues to walk away. He sits down at his desk with a sigh as he gently taps his fingertips on top of the black keyboard on his desk. He swiftly sits up pushing his glasses up on his nose and then begins to rapidly type on the keyboard, staring at the computer screen with determination. After several hours Ki-ha leans back in his chair with a disappointed sigh rubbing the palms of his hands using his thumbs. He glances at his watch and grabs his jacket as he stands up and leaves.

Lightly knocking before he opens the door, Ki-ha walks into Min-jah's office.

"Sir." he says with a bow. "It's time for the board meeting."

Glancing up Ki-ha notices Min-jah wasn't at his desk. Quickly looking around he sees Min-jah kneeling on the floor next to the couch. He quietly walks over to see Joon was fast asleep on the couch. Min-jah takes off his coat and gently drapes it across the shoulders of the sleeping Joon. Ki-ha smiles lightly as he stands and watches Min-jah softly stroke the back of Joon's head.

"Are you ready Sir?" Ki-ha reluctantly interrupts quietly.

"Yeah." Min-jah says with a sigh as he stands up.

Swiftly walking down the corridor to the meeting room Ki-ha pulls out a tablet and hands it to Min-jah.

"Have you found out anything on that number I gave you?" Min-jah asks while looking through the contents on the tablet.

"I only wish to update you when I have good news." Ki-ha says dejectedly.

"That's fine, I want to know exactly where you are in your investigation at all times." he demands.

"Yes Sir. Unfortunately the number is from a burner phone and although it was activated recently, it was purchased from a convenience store over eighteen months ago. All surveillance video is long gone so I do not have a face of this man. Yet." Ki-ha says as they walk up to the meeting room door.

"Keep at it." Min-jah commands pushing the door open.

"Yes Sir." Ki-ha says with a bow as Min-jah walks in.

Sitting at the small round table surrounded by employees nervously and excitedly chattering Seon slowly lifts her hand to silence the room.

"I'm sure word has already spread throughout the whole building that Chairman Lan did in fact come in this morning with a very special guest." She says in a serious tone.

"I heard they were holding hands the whole time!" someone interjects quickly.

Seon quickly darts a strong glare in the direction of the voice before releasing a sigh.

"After the debacle with Byung-woo I feel like this is just a stunt to draw attention in another direction." she says calmly.

The crowd mumbles with waves of agreement and some protest as she stands up from the table.

"Ladies and gentlemen I don't believe he is gay." she states confidently.

With scattered agreements most employees rolled their eyes as they filed out of the room. After that day Min-jah took me to get a new phone with a whole new number I stopped receiving messages. It's been three months since I've been coming to work with Min-jah every day and for the most part it is like he said aside from the daily board meetings he is working in his office right next to me. And although I had a clean bill of health from my doctor both Min-jah and Mr. Wei refused to let me return to work.

Glancing over at the empty desk I put down the book I was reading. Sighing softly I looked around the empty office before standing up and walking toward the door. Slowly pushing the door open I peeked out to see all the employees rushing about the office making phone calls or copying papers. I made my way slowly down the hall staying out of the way the best I could.

I quickly dashed inside an open door as an employee with an arm full of papers headed my way. Catching my breath I looked around to find myself in an empty office. Under the window looking out toward the floor were small two drawer filing cabinets that lined the front wall, there were two large bookcases against the wall filled with books on either side of the wooden desk that was directly in the center of the room. With two chairs placed in front I saw a nameplate that read 'Kim Ki-ha' sitting at the edge of the desk. On the back wall there were taller filing cabinets that had small plants on the top of them.

I walked around the desk to see the top littered with all kinds of paperwork. On the computer screen a program was quickly searching through a database with pictures flashing too quickly to get a clear look. Confused I turned my attention to a yellow folder that was labeled 'Kim Byung-woo's properties' that was laying under a layer of paper on the desk. I pulled the folder out knocking some papers on to the floor and opened it to see an extensive list and information of properties. Some of the names were crossed out with the single word 'no' written next to it. I turned the page to see a name circled many times with the words 'he's here' written next to it. The name that was circled was the name of the water treatment plant Byung-woo had me held captive at.

Noticing a blue notebook where the folder had been I closed the folder. Placing the folder down I slowly picked up and opened the notebook. Unable to stop them tears rolled down my face as I read what was written on the pages. Inside starting with my name was a list of things about me starting with my date of birth, all the terrible things people had done to me, and a list of all my favorite things. Turning page after page everything written had something to do with me. There were diary entries written, in between the data compiled about me, and dated for the days I was in the coma. Someone writing as if the only thing they desperately wanted was for me to wake up and talk to them. I slowly turned page after page to find the words 'I must protect him' written so darkly as if the words had been traced over a million times.

"Chairman Lan gave me that the day you finally woke up." Ki-ha said.

Startled by his voice I quickly dropped the notebook back on the desk as I wiped the tears off my face.

"He wrote in that notebook every night, religiously I might add, while sitting next to you in the hospital. He gave it to me in hopes that I could learn something from it and possibly become friends with you. Although I'm still working on that one thing I did learn from it is that you are an extremely important person to Chairman Lan. And just like the last sentence in that notebook states I will protect Chairman Lan but in order to do that I must protect you." Ki-ha says standing in the doorway.

I wiped more tears off my face staring at Ki-ha in the doorway as a soft grin slowly appeared on his face.

"Come on the board meeting is over already he will be looking for you." Ki-ha says softly as he extends his hand toward the doorway.

Min-jah quickly walks out of his office looking around sighing with relief as he sees Joon walking toward him with Ki-ha. Ki-ha glances up giving him a small nod as they walk closer. Relieved Min-jah turns around and goes back into his office with a smile.

I stretched with a loud groan as I turned to look at Min-jah still working hard at his desk. I sighed with a smile as he glanced up at me. I looked down at the watch on my wrist to see it was already almost 10PM.

"Alright time to go home." Min-jah says ecstatic closing the last binder.

"Okay." I replied, closing my book.

Gathering up our things Min-jah extends his hand out with a smile as I meet him in the center of the room. Grabbing his hand Ki-ha suddenly bursts into the room with a concerned look on his face. Looking at each other we reluctantly let each other's hands go with a sigh.

"Sorry Sir there's been an incident at one of the protest locations. An emergency board meeting has been called." Ki-ha spits out in a rush.

"Okay, let's go." Min-jah sighs out.

Ki-ha bows and immediately leaves the room. Min-jah turns towards me with an apologetic expression.

"It's okay, I'll just wait here." I say with a smile.

Min-jah smiles at me sweetly before pulling me into a hug.

"I'll try to make it quick." he says as he quickly kissed my forehead.

"Go on, go to work." I say with a chuckle pushing him toward the door.

He groans in contempt as he reluctantly walks through the door. Chuckling softly I toss my jacket over the back of the couch and sit back down. Sighing I close my eyes and lean my head back.

Hours later a loud thud coming from outside the office doors startled me awake. Not sure when I fell asleep I quickly got up to go look. Sitting on the floor in the dark was Seon rubbing her ankle.

"What are you still doing here?" I ask as I walk towards her.

"As long as Chairman Lan is in the office, I have to be too." she groans rubbing her ankle.

"What happened?" I ask as I kneel down next to her.

"I tripped and twisted my ankle on my way to go get coffee for everyone." she winces as I touch her foot.

"Doesn't look too bad but you shouldn't walk on it. Let me go get you some ice." I say standing back up.

Quickly grabbing a towel and some ice I returned to the injured Seon. Pulling up a chair for her to sit on and another to elevate her foot I carefully place the towel with the ice over her ankle.

"Ugh... what about the coffee?" she groans.

"Don't worry about it I'll go get it." I said.

"Really?" she swooned.

"Yeah it shouldn't be that hard." I chuckled.

"Awe you are a lifesaver here take this." she said as she handed me a credit card.

I smiled as I took it out of her hand and turned to walk away.

"Oh! This too!" she quickly added giving me her employee badge. "The guard at the gate would have already gone home for the night so you will need this to open them."

"Right." I said as I took the lanyard from her.

I rushed to the elevator hitting the lobby button as soon as I was inside. Darting across the lobby I quickly pushed the doors open leaving the building.

Standing in the shadows he shifted slightly as the movement in front of the building caught his attention. Sniffling he watched as the young man who just exited made his way from the door to the crosswalk up the street. He smiled as he stood up from his hiding spot and made his way to join the small group of people at the crosswalk. Standing right behind Joon he could feel his heart beating faster as he slowly raised his hand up. Inching his hand closer he reached out to grab the back of Joon's clothes when the light suddenly turned green. Instantly bolting across the street the target of his grasp quickly goes out of reach. Watching him run into the coffee shop on the corner the man stops following him.

The barista sets four drink holders and two large bags of food on the counter.

"Here's your order." she says with a smile.

I stared appalled that they would actually send a petite girl to carry all this back to the office alone. Shaking my head I started to grab everything. Placing the last bag right on top of the mountain of drinks I slowly made my way to the door. I lean back against the door to push it open when someone quickly grabs the door.

"Oh thank you!" I say with a smile to the gentleman who held the door open for me.

I quickly made my way back to the crosswalk where I struggled to hit the button and not drop anything at the same time. Still shook that all those men in that room would send one tiny girl to carry all this back I stepped into the street hearing a small ding thinking the light had turned green.

"Hey!" a voice shouts behind me.

They quickly grabbed the collar of my clothes pulling me back on the sidewalk as a car honked their horn while driving by.

"Oh I'm so sorry. Thank you!" I say turning toward the person.

Standing there was a man with black eyes that matched his short jet black hair and pale white skin. Wearing a dark brown coat, black leather gloves, blue jeans, and a black baseball cap he stood there staring at me.

"It's nothing, just pay attention." he scolded.

"Right sorry." I agreed, embarrassed turning away from him.

The light turned green and I swiftly made my way across. I rounded the corner into the driveway when a black gloved hand quickly slides across my face. I was suddenly reminded of the whole reason I was even going to the office with Min-jah in the first place. I instantly dropped everything in my hands and began to struggle against the hand pulling me backward. Wincing from a sudden pinch on the side of my neck I struggled harder making the syringe fall out of his hand. My body began to feel heavy as the syringe clattered under my feet as I struggled to fight back losing consciousness.

Turning the corner Ki-ha saw Seon sitting with her leg propped up on a chair. He swiftly walks over to her.

"What happened?" he asks sharply.

"I tripped and twisted my ankle." she explained.

"Well why didn't you have Mr. Park-Chul come tell me?" he asks.

"Well he went to go get the coffee." she said nonchalantly.

"He what? How long ago?" he quickly asks.

"Like fifteen minutes ago?" she guessed.

He instantly rushes toward the elevator pressing the button rapidly. As soon as the doors opened he rushed in pressing the lobby button. Flying out of the elevator he jumped over the security gates and dashed outside. Panicked he looked all around until he noticed all the spilt coffee and doughnuts on the ground. Rushing over he finds Seon's employee badge and a broken syringe on the ground next to the mess quickly looking around he groans before grabbing his head in frustration.

The elevator door opens with a ding as Ki-ha calmly walks out. He slowly makes his way through the office back toward Seon.

"Where's Joon with the coffee?" Seon asks puzzled.

Ki-ha promptly tosses her her employee badge as he walks past without saying a word.

He walks briskly almost at a run as he rushes down the long corridor leading to the meeting room. Bursting through the door loudly he composes himself before immediately walking over to the head of the table. Confused, the men around the table begin to nervously whisper amongst each other as Ki-ha quickly makes his way to Min-jah. He leans down and starts to quickly talk in a hushed whisper. Min-jah flashes a quick expression of shock before instantly hardening as the words continue to flow out of Ki-ha's mouth. His head down he crumples the papers that were in his hand as Ki-ha finishes whispering. Min-jah glances upward with a hardened stare as Ki-ha slowly stands back up.

To be continued...

CPSIA information can be obtained
at www.ICGtesting.com
Printed in the USA
BVHW031443030720
582914BV00001B/123

9 781984 584687